Best Wishes

Mike Tolbert

THREE DAYS IN AUGUST

MIKE HOLST

iUniverse®

THREE DAYS IN AUGUST

iUniverse
1663 Liberty Drive
Bloomington, IN 47403
www.iuniverse.com
1-800-Authors (1-800-288-4677)

ISBN: 978-1-4917-7048-1 (sc)
ISBN: 978-1-4917-7049-8 (e)

iUniverse rev. date: 06/16/2015

ALSO BY MIKE HOLST

A long Way Back

Nothing to Lose

Justice For Adam

No Clues in the Ashes

Back to the Ashes

The Magic Book

The Last Trip Down the Mountain

An Absence of Conscience

Coming Home at Last

Visions of Justice

ACKNOWLEDGMENTS

To my readers who always seem to encourage me and make me want to try and write that "best book of all."

To Pat McCormick. Always there for me, always willing to help and my fiercest critic who spent countless hours, to help me get it right.

CHAPTER ONE

High on a hill, over looking the confluence of the Wapsipinicon and Bitter Rivers, Samuel Morton squinted into the afternoon sun and gazed intently over the vast prairie land of east central Iowa territory. He was mesmerized by what lay before him and because of this self induced trance and the dreams he had, he was oblivious to the hardships and dangers that came with life in the territory. The Year was 1844, the month was June, and Sam and his small family had migrated west from the Ohio valley to start a new life. His wife Emma sat passively on the wagon seat, nursing her one year old son Brandon, and not sharing his enthusiasm, but at the same time totally subservient to her husband's dreams for a new life. Four-year-old David slept fitfully in the back, in a pile of quilts. He had been cooped up in the wagon for far too long, and yearned to run and play as he once had back in Ohio.

Samuel had been attracted to the area by the offer of free land; next to the proposed railroad rite-a-way and this along with his dissatisfaction with politics and crowding, back in the Ohio valley, had made him pack and move. He sold his farm, loaded his possessions into his new covered wagon and started west over a month ago. The trip had been easy at first, passing through towns and hamlets in civilized Indiana and Illinois, but the farther west he had gone, the more the trail narrowed and about a hundred miles back, after crossing the Mississippi, it and most of the people had disappeared completely. Now as he stood quietly, he decided he had gone far enough. Seemingly hypnotized by the scenery in front of him, he tethered his horses to a tree and walked down the steep river bank, cupped his hands and tasted the clear bubbling waters. As far as the eye could see the prairie was wide open with a sea of tall green grass, gently bending in the westerly breezes almost inviting him to stay. A white tail deer curiously eyed him from the opposite river bank and then just as quickly as it had appeared, turn and ran back into the brush. In the waters in front of him, fish teemed in schools swimming lazily against the current, seemingly suspended in the translucent waters.

Abundant water, wild game and fertile land, this place seemed to have it all, and at least in his mind there was no need to press on farther. Samuel knew this was only the start of the vast Midwest prairie land, but fear of the unknown and the presence of the Sioux Indians had made him somewhat cautious about going any farther west. He turned and walked back up the bank to Emma. His voice was soft but firm as he took her limp hand and said. "This is it Emma, our new home. We will build, settle and be here when the railroad comes through."

This land had once been home to the Iowa Indians, the proud tribe that the territory had been named after. They had migrated south from Canada and Minnesota, were they'd found the buffalo in vast herds that dotted the plains, and the indigenous people hunted them for their hides and meat. They were also skilled farmers and grew many different crops in the fertile ground of the plains of Eastern Iowa. By the early eighteen hundreds though, they were gone, the victims of disease and the white man. The Sioux who came later were mostly gone too, having drifted back to the Minnesota territories, but there were still pockets of them here and there. Just enough to keep a lone white man alert and honest.

For over two years Samuel and Emma toiled, building their new home and watching with pride as their children and their new homestead grew. The Indians seemed to accept them and other settlers slowly moved into the fertile river valley. Emma seemed at peace once more, with herself and her destiny. The first winter had been kind to them, at a time when they had been unprepared for what it might have been. The second winter had been harsh and long, but by this time they were no strangers to this kind of hardship and they hunkered down and rode it out.

In 1846 the Iowa territory became a state, with little towns and hamlets springing up everywhere as more and more people came west and beyond. Samuel laid claim to over a thousand acres and his herd of cattle was growing with every passing year. This was also the year his brother

Billy arrived with his family and set up house, a stones throw from Samuel, Emma and their two sons. Samuel had also acquired some crude farm implements on his many trips to Iowa City, and in the spring of forty- six he broke the ground and planted corn and other grains that flourished in the rich loamy soil, providing food to feed his family and his growing herd of cattle.

Emma grew vegetables and fruits, carefully tending her garden, canning and preserving them for next winter's siege. They had moved into their new log home and the temporary one they had spent the first year and a half in was now turned into the barn. It was a rough lonely life at first for Emma. She had left all of her family behind in Ohio and the occasional letters she would get when Samuel went to Iowa City, was her only contact with the outside world. Samuel had little time for Emma and the children as he worked from sunup to sundown. Somehow despite the lack of attention, she did find herself pregnant in the fall of forty-six. The baby would be due in March as near as she could figure. With Billy's family of seven there would now be twelve of them in the immediate family in what was now being called Morton's Valley.

In the spring of 1847 Emma gave birth to a baby girl delivered by Billy's wife Dorothy but the infant lived only for a few hours. Samuel carved a headstone out of hemlock and his daughter became the first occupant in the new Morton valley cemetery. A traveling preacher who had come from Iowa City had a service for the baby and then decided to hang around for a while to attend to Emma and try to convert some of the settlers around the countryside. In the spring of 48 he broke ground for his newfound flock and Morton Valley had its first church. At abut this same time, Isaac Newberry came to the valley and started a small general store on land Samuel provided and the first railroad spur was announced, coming into Morton Valley.

Settlers came and went with more of them coming than going and by the time the civil war broke out, the town could lay claim to over a hundred souls. Samuel and Emma's son David was the first to leave to fight for the union. Eighteen years old and a big strapping man, he kissed his tearful Mother goodbye shook his fathers hand and disappeared for three years.

Emma had never gotten over the death of her infant daughter and the subsequent infertility it had left her with. She had wanted many babies for Samuel but it was not to be, so she turned her attention to her sons and fourteen years later was heartbroken to see David leave, firmly believing she would never see him again. David did return in the fall of 1864 with a new wife, a child and a new generation of Morton's. He was just in time to take over the reigns of the ranch and Morton Valley from Samuel who was dying of tuberculosis.

Samuel lived until 1884 and then he was buried in the small cemetery next to his infant daughter and about ten other souls. Emma moved in with David and his family until her death in the spring of 1891.

David's brother Brandon worked the farm along with his brother. Brandon never married although he had several lady friends and the word around town was he just preferred to be alone. David knew his brothers secret about his homosexuality and when Brandon would leave to go to the city from time to time he would explain his absence as business. Brandon always came back and in his heart David knew that it would just be a mater of time before his secret did get out and then he would disappear for good. By this time David's five sons and three daughters were starting families of their own with most of them staying in the area.

Morton valley by the early turn of the century was a bustling farming community of eight hundred and it seemed that every day, something new would come along. There were the first steam tractors and threshing machines. Automobiles would be a few years later, but people had seen them in Iowa City and it was just a matter of time.

The first national bank of Morton was chartered. There were now two saloons and a café. Three general stores and a grain elevator, along with a livery stable and a blacksmith shop. There was a Catholic Church brought in by some missionary priests and the very first elementary school was established. Morton valley was very much on the map and here to stay. Along with all of the progress came the growing pains every small town experiences. Drunkenness and prostitution seemed to head the list. There just wasn't a lot to do in your leisure time in Morton Valley. The law had to come all the way from Iowa City so there was not much of that to contend with either.

The Wapsipinicon and the Bitter Rivers still flowed each and every day but the waters were now more often than not, muddy and filled with runoff from the fields and pastures. The fish had moved elsewhere as did the deer and other forest animals. The forestlands that had existed along the riverbanks had long ago been cut for lumber and firewood. The bountiful land that Samuel had settled almost seventy years ago had changed dramatically.

In 1910 both David and Brandon died with in months of each other but the Morton name was still the most prevalent name in town. They stuck together, brother's sisters and cousins. They rarely gossiped about each other and had few disagreements; it was as if they had a code of ethics they all lived by. Two boys went away to World War I in 1918 and one came back a hero. The other was buried in France the only Morton that people could think of that was not buried on the hill behind Samuels original cabin, which now had been taken over by the Catholic Church.

The great depression seemed to not have much effect on the town, they just cinched up their belts and carried on and then came along World War II and three more Morton's served overseas with only one coming back. Jack David Morton. Jack was a decorated marine who had fought in some of the fiercest battles of the Pacific theatre. Jack was also David's oldest grandchild and after the war he became the new self proclaimed patriarch of the Morton family. He was president of the Morton State Bank, drove a big black Packard automobile and built his wife Thelma and children, a huge brick mansion on the highest hill in town. Jack and his overly pretentious wife had three sons and a daughter. The oldest son Jack Jr. worked in the bank with his father and the middle one Clyde went farming. Their daughter Maria married a rich kid from Iowa City and didn't come home more than once a year. The youngest son Teddy however was the real problem child and that's really what this story is all about.

CHAPTER TWO

MAY 5, 1959

From the time he was born in June of 1943, Theodore, or Teddy Morton as he preferred to be called, was a problem. No, actually he was more than a problem; he was a royal pain in the ass. As a baby he drove his mother nuts with his colic and hissy fits. He never slept more than three hours at once, bawled about everything, and would only eat ice cream and sweets, spiting anything else back in the face of who ever was feeding him. He hated baby sitters and his father, refusing to obey anyone but his mother, and then, only when he felt like it. As a toddler he didn't potty train until he was five and even then he would crap his pants from time to time just to let the others know he was still in charge of that.

The public school system asked that he be sent somewhere else by the time he was in the third grade, and his father enrolled him in the Catholic school even though they weren't Catholic. It took some very generous donations to the parish to keep him there. He was constantly fighting with the other kids and when he was not fighting, he was exposing himself on the playground, to some girls or swearing at the nuns.

When it came time to graduate from the Catholic school, at the end of the eighth grade, the parish could only breathe a sigh of relief. Nobody needed the money that bad.

There was no high school in Morton Valley and all of the kids were bussed to Perkins Prairie which was about thirty miles away. Perkins Prairie was a town of about ten thousand and the county seat of Perkins County. That is all the kids were bused there except Teddy who was thrown off the bus the first day of school for trying to sexually molest a girl on the way to school and getting into fisticuffs with the bus driver when he interceded on the girls behalf. So Jack had to drive Teddy to Perkins Prairie each morning before he went to the bank. A chore he hated, and the trip was more times than not, dominated by some fights and verbal bashing of his wayward son that only exasperated the many problems Teddy had, and deepened his hatred for his father.

Teddy was not a small child; in fact he had been overweight most of his life and weighed over two hundred and fifty pounds at age fifteen. That coupled with the fact that he preferred to be filthy and unkempt, also made him pretty much of a slob in most peoples eyes. If you were poor and could not help it, people could overlook that, but the son of one of the richest men in town. Well that was unforgivable in Morton Valley.

He had long black stringy hair, which he wore down to his shoulders and seldom washed. He had a bad case of acne to go along with his grungy look and he refused medical care for his skin problem. His favorite mode of dress was bib overalls, white tee shirts and filthy old tennis shoes filled with holes. He was chain smoking when he was thirteen, drank any kind of alcohol he could get his hands on, and had been seen urinating and exposing himself in public many times. Teddy was just a total embarrassment to his family, and the people of Morton Valley and anyone who knew him. But Teddy wasn't embarrassed by any of this. Make no mistake about it; he loved the role he played. The more trouble he could get in, the more trouble he would dream up to get involved with.

For Jack and Thelma they had reached a point of giving up completely. They had tried everything known to man, but nothing seemed to work with their belligerent son. They spent thousands of dollars on therapy and psychiatrist's and they all came to the same conclusion. Teddy was incorrigible and a born troublemaker. Both Jack and Thelma had been told by friends and neighbors that Teddy needed to be locked up somewhere and the key should be thrown away before he hurt someone or worse. So on that day in 1959 when he ran away from home one more time---basically his father was more relieved than sad. Thelma however was sad but kept it to herself.

It had been late afternoon when Teddy arrived in Iowa City that fifth day of April. He had hitched a ride outside of Morton Valley, and a sympathetic farmer had picked him up, but only if he rode in the back of the pickup with the dog. Teddy didn't mind however, the dog was friendly and probably better company than that nosey old man would have been anyway. The old man had watched him suspiciously in the rear view mirror most of the way from Morton Valley. He was having second thoughts about picking him up, but was feeling somewhat secure with the big guy in the box in the back, and just to be safe he locked the cab doors. He stopped at a railroad crossing stop sign and peered down the tracks for trains and that was the last he saw of Teddy, as he bailed out over the side of the truck and disappeared in the rail yards. No thanks or even a wave but that was all right. Good riddance.

CHAPTER THREE

The steel wheels of the boxcar clicked on every coupling they ran over on the rails as the freight train slowly made its way out of Iowa City heading west to Denver. Teddy sat in the doorway of an empty Northern Pacific boxcar and watched the buildings of the city become fewer and fewer, and then at last, there was only freshly planted fields of corn and alfalfa to stare at. He could smell the rich, loamy, recently turned over soil as they passed by it. It made him think of the country around Morton Valley and for a second he wondered if running away was going to solve anything but he quickly dismissed the thought.

He had an old, tattered red gym bag, sitting beside him as his only luggage. It held some spare socks and underwear, two cartons of Lucky Strikes and a quart of bourbon he had stolen from his father's liquor cabinet. There were also three cans of spam, a half of a loaf of bread and a bag of cookies. His mother never cooked so there wasn't much food in the house to take. He had taken all of the money he could find in the house, which wasn't much. One hundred and three dollars, the last time he counted it, most of it from his mother's purse, she had carelessly left on the kitchen table. He had stolen so much over the years that his parents rarely left money around anywhere. He also had a small transistor radio and a kitchen knife about eight inches long for protection. It was wrapped in a sock right on top of the bag.

The inside of the boxcar smelled like soybeans and there were still a few of them scattered around on the wooden floor. There were also some sheets of cardboard that had been used to line the walls, piled in the end to his left. The wind coming in the door blew them around from time to time but there was no place for them to go, so they just kind of flapped up and down. The boxcar had doors on both sides, but the one he was sitting in was the only one open. Teddy had hopped freights before for transportation but usually just for a thrill ride and usually only on flat bed cars where he could see what was on them. There were a lot of hobos that rode the rails and he wanted no part of meeting up with one in an enclosed boxcar. If the train stopped, he had made plans to close the door.

Although the train was on its way to Denver, Teddy had no idea where he was going and he didn't care. Any place had to be better than Morton Valley. The train slowed many times during the day for small towns, and once pulled off on a siding to let faster trains pass by but rarely stopped or slowed enough for Teddy to jump off, if he had been so inclined. He wasn't inclined and nothing had looked inviting so far anyway. When they went around wide curves in the tracks he could see the three big black diesel units, up front, belching smoke as they pulled their heavy cargo. He could also see the little red caboose in the back. He knew there were people in both of them to avoid but he was in the middle of a long train. His instincts told him that if he couldn't make out anybody back there, they couldn't see him either. Teddy was getting bored and irritated with the incessant blowing of the whistle at every country crossing and for a long time he sat with his index fingers in his ears to drown out the noise and finally he gave up and retreated to the farthest corner of the boxcar, opposite the cardboard piles and took a long pull off his bourbon bottle. It warmed him up a little and calmed him down. It was getting cold and dark and some of his bravado was wearing off. This was a far cry from the warm bed he was used to at home. A few more drinks and he fell asleep, propped up in the corner of the car.

When he woke up he could see the first vestiges of a new day dawning out the open boxcar door. The train seemed to have picked up speed and the cars were lurching and bouncing more on the tracks. The side of his head was sore from bouncing on the hard wood wall of the boxcar throughout the night and his back and neck ached from being bent in one position to long. His hand was still griping the half empty bourbon bottle and he stuffed it back in his gym bag, found his cigarettes and lit one. His mouth was dry and almost sore and he was mad at himself for not bringing along something to drink besides the bourbon. On top of this, he had to pee badly.

Teddy pulled himself up into a unsteady standing position and stood leaning against the end wall for a brief moment. He was dizzy from his hangover so he walked along the wall; hand over hand toward the open door. At the door he peered out at the countryside. There were no more farm fields to be seen just miles and miles of brown prairie grass. The terrain seemed to be more rolling than yesterday and he had the feeling that they were gradually going up hill, more than down. Were they still in Iowa, and what state was west of Iowa? Teddy scratched his head to try and make his foggy mind come to focus.

His original intention was to pee out the open door but he was too unsteady and the car lurching back and forth made it difficult to stand, even holding on with both hands. He went to the far end of the car where he had been sitting; leaned facing the wall extracted his unit and peed on the floor. Maybe as long as he had used this end for his toilet he would get his bag and go to the other end of the car for a while and sit on the cardboard pile. Anything to cushion his ass from this constant bouncing and beating it was taking.

Two things were first and foremost in Teddy's mind. He had to get off this damn train and find some water, and he had to also find out where the hell he was. Not that it would help him to know anyway. It just pissed him off not knowing where he was heading. He thought it was Montana because they seemed to be going west as the sun was coming up opposite of where they were heading. Hungry, Teddy tore into his cookie supply but ate only part of one throwing the rest at the other end of the car. He needed a drink of water before he could eat anything that dry. He stared at the wet spot on the floor where he had peed and it only served to make him thirstier.

Now it seemed to be getting colder out and from time to time Teddy could see snow in the ditches. All the snow in Iowa had been gone over a month ago. He decided to sandwich himself between several layers of cardboard to try and stay warm. He did have on a warm, but tattered flannel shirt, but no jacket. He wasn't very well prepared for this journey but that was the story of Teddy's life.

Teddy took another hit on the bourbon bottle. It wasn't that he needed a drink but he did need something wet and this was all he had. The first drink went down hard but before long it was hitting the spot and Teddy was well on his way to another drunken stupor. He was getting tired again but he was also getting relaxed again and horny. He put his hand in his pocket and felt himself getting aroused. *That would warm him up; he would just lie here and play with himself for a while. He should have brought one of his magazines along for entertainment.* He was well on his way to accomplishing what his wandering oversexed mind could conjure up for fantasy thoughts, when the car suddenly lurched sideways knocking him off balance and ruining his whole train of thought. Damn *engineer where the hell did he learn how to drive a train.*

He crawled over to the door on his hands and knees and looked outside. There had been only one other track that he knew of on the whole trip out here right outside his open door. Trains going the other direction were constantly going by but now there were two other tracks. Something else was strange the train was slowing down and he could smell cow shit. *Yes he had lived around enough cattle to know that smell, but where the hell were the cows? There was nothing out there but dead grass and a few scrubby trees.*

He crawled to the other side of the car and slid the door back about an inch. *Cattle pens built right beside the track's full of Hereford beef cattle just like his damn brother raised.* It was all coming together for Teddy. The train was barely crawling now and the car he was in was already beyond the cattle pens. Now he saw people and men on horses riding between the pens sliding gates open and herding them into chutes that faced the tracks. Just then the train lurched to a stop

For a few minutes all Teddy did was peer back and into the cattle pens. Then he heard boxcar doors opening, on cattle cars down at the other end of the train and saw the men positioning the chutes to load the cattle onto the train. The two men in the caboose had come forward walking alongside the train. One of then was signaling the engineer with hand signals from time to time and the train would move up one boxcar at a time.

Something else had caught Teddy's attention. Two pickup trucks parked almost in front of him on a gravel road. He could steal one of those trucks and get the hell out of here if the keys were in them. He would drive to the next town and ditch the truck and get some water. What if they spotted him and chased him? He had no idea where he was or where the next town was. But he couldn't just sit here in this damn boxcar and freeze to death or die of thirst.

Teddy lowered himself to the ground, out the wide open door on the opposite side of the train from all of the activity. He crawled under the train and watched. The trucks were now about a hundred feet back. The train started to move ahead again so he made a dash for it down the embankment, through the ditch, heading for the trucks. The first truck was an old blue ford custom. The box was filled with hay bales and a saddle. Teddy opened the door slowly; as the hinges squeaked but the cattle were making so much noise they would never hear him. Looking inside he saw no keys; just an empty cab but there was a rifle in a rack behind the seat. That might come in handy. He reached up and took it down and closed the door and went on to the other truck. No keys again. Just a black dinner pail and a gallon Igloo cooler. Teddy opened the little spigot and cool water ran out. After quenching his thirst he sat down in the ditch to think. Maybe stealing the truck was not such a good idea. He would just take the water, the dinner pail and the rifle and hope that his ride got going again before they came back to the trucks. Teddy crawled back up to the tracks and rolled under the train and out the other side. His boxcar was now about three hundred feet away because the train had moved several times in the time he had been gone. He ran to the open door, threw his newfound bounty inside and crawled in. Then he went to the other side of the car and looked back at the pens. Almost all of the cattle had been loaded and the two men from the caboose were walking back to it. The men who were loading the cattle, while on their horses seemed to still be busy. The train moved once more and then he heard brakes hissing and the train lurched forward again, but this time it kept going. There were on their way. Where to? He had no idea, but he did have more food, water and a rifle to protect him.

CHAPTER FOUR

Jack Morton stood in his son's bedroom doorway, in his striped boxers, scratching his crotch and rubbing his eyes. "Thelma. You got any idea where Teddy is?" Thelma appeared beside Jack, clutching her robe to her bosom.

"He didn't say anything to me about going somewhere. I do wonder where he is," she replied with a worried look on her face?

"You know Thelma as much as I should say-- I give a shit, I don't, and not having to haul his sorry ass to school today makes me even happier."

"Jack. How you talk, he's your son."

"Not any more he isn't. We should have traded that little bastard for a mangy dog when he was a baby and shot the dog like people have said." Jack turned and walked back to his bedroom.

"I have an early meeting this morning with the mayor Thelma. It seems the city wants to float a loan from us dear, for a new public safety building."

Thelma had come back in the bedroom and was sitting on the end of the bed. "So that is more important than your son's whereabouts."

Jack looked at her clearly annoyed. "What the hell I am I supposed to do about it Thelma. This isn't the first time that fat ass has run off and it won't be the last time." Jack maybe looked annoyed, but he put his hand on her shoulder while he looked in the mirror and straightened his tie, bent over and kissed her forehead. Don't worry dear he'll come home when he gets hungry. Just look at the fat slob, he's always hungry."

Jack grabbed his suit coat and was out the door and down the stairs. Thelma sat on the end of the bed until she heard his car back out of the garage and drive away. Then she crawled back in bed and sobbed in her pillow. *How could Jack be so cruel to his own flesh and blood? True, Teddy was a problem but Jack's indifference toward him didn't help anything.*

14

The train seemed to be going much faster now than it had been. Teddy was sitting on the pile of cardboard admiring his newfound rifle. He sighted down the barrel and pulled the trigger. There was an ear splitting roar and splintered wood flew off the end wall of the boxcar.

"Holy shit," Teddy screamed, and then went into a fit of laughter. "The bastard was loaded," he yelled.

He ejected the shell and put a fresh one in the chamber. Then he laid the gun down and opened the dinner pail he had stolen

There was a sandwich wrapped in wax paper and he unwrapped and opened it. Egg salad and it smelled so good. He ate the rest of the lunch and then noticed a newspaper folded up and stuffed in the lid. Teddy unfolded it and opened it up. Winthrop Nebraska Weekly Gazette.

Teddy scratched his head. *Shit he thought he was in Montana, not Nebraska. Hell, who went to Nebraska? What the hell came after Nebraska? Montana had to be next. Goddamn, it was getting colder by the minute,* and now he could make out mountains in the distance. He reached for the rest of the bourbon.

Jack was in his glory talking to the city council and the mayor in the bank conference room. They had all been treated to a buffet breakfast that was set up along one wall of the lavishly furnished room. Now all of them, full of food and drinking hot gourmet coffee, listened carefully to Jacks presentation.

"Morton Valley First National has always been ready to help this great city gentleman. My great, great grandfather carved this town out of the dusty prairie over a hundred and twenty years ago and our family recognizes the obligation we have to keep this town growing, isn't that right son." Jack looked down at his oldest son Jack Jr., who smiled and nodded in the affirmative.

"We're not only going to grant that loan, we are going to give it to you interest free. All we ask in return is your careful consideration, in the matter of the Bank of Benton opening up a branch office here in Morton, which I have heard they are trying to do. You see gentleman this is a small town and not big enough for two banks. I'm not saying they would drive us out of business but we could never make such a lucrative offer, if we had to share the business we have." Jack seemed to have a pained expression on his face as he looked at each and every member of the council. Most of them nodded in agreement and he wisely dropped the subject.

Thelma had not forgotten about her wayward son but she had managed to put it in the back of her mind. She had to get her hair fixed this morning and then she was invited for a tea at the Ladies Aid Society of their church. She had been invited to speak on the subject of having a loving family. What does it take? She and Jack had been chosen as role models. *Maybe she could talk about hypocrites too,* she thought.

It was getting colder by the minute and now instead of sporadic sightings of snow banks, there seemed to be snow everywhere. Also those mountains that had been on the horizon a few hours ago, well now they were in them. Teddy stared out of the door from across the car, reclining in his cardboard mound. Just his head was sticking out and he was shivering violently. He had to get off this train and soon, before he froze to death, but not out here in the middle of nowhere.

He had drunk the rest of the bourbon and threw the empty bottle out of the door along with the lunch box he had stolen from the truck. Teddy was having second thoughts about the comfortable life he had left, but he couldn't go back now. He would have to kiss his fathers ass and things would have to get a whole lot worse before that was going to happen. He did miss his Mom though, and maybe he would call her when he found a place to stay. For now he had his hand back in his pocket playing with himself once more. *He needed to get laid someday and find out what it was really like to be with a woman. He had seen very few women naked, and actually had never even seen a real vagina. Oh he had peeked at his sister getting undressed, but there was just too much hair in the way to see anything. Yes when he got his chance he was going to go down there on some gal somewhere, someday and get a first hand look at that place all the boys were always talking about.*

Teddy had slept for awhile, helped along by the booze and when he awoke it was dusk but a glance out the door told him something had changed and he crawled from his cardboard bed and went to the open door. There were lots of houses and streetlights going by. Traffic on the road parallel to the tracks was heavy and the train appeared to be slowing. There was still just one other train track on the right but a trip to the other door showed many sets of tracks. They were coming into a big rail yard. The train was going slow enough now that he could jump off, but he was still wasn't comfortable, or sure that this was the time and the place. Once off, there would be no getting back on. If the train speeded up again he would be out of luck. They had to be somewhere in Montana.

Suddenly the train lurched changing tracks again and they were on the outside track, heading around a big curve. It appeared that this was the only track going this way and the train had slowed almost to a crawl parked along side of a long row of buildings with loading docks next to the track. There was a familiar smell in the air right now but his foggy mind couldn't place it. It was time to disembark.

Teddy stood and looked at the rifle. How was he going to take that and remain inconspicuous and yet he didn't want to leave it behind in case the train left. He would have to hide it outside somewhere for the time being. He grabbed his old gym bag, jumped down and then reached back into the boxcar for the rifle. He had wrapped it up in a piece of cardboard to hide it the best he could. His legs were wobbly from all of the riding, but he managed to jog along the track for a while and ducked into what appeared to be an auto salvage yard. He could see a fire going in a rusty steel barrel not far away, and the shadowy forms of at least two men warming their hands over the fire. Teddy stayed behind an old truck and tried to scope out the area better, before someone saw him. They had to be hobos. He had heard about hobos that rode the rails going from town to town, begging for food or money. *Might not be that bad of life except for the begging part,* he thought. *Maybe if I just kind of sauntered up to them they could tell me where I was at and where the nearest store was so I could buy some food. I could give them a can of spam just to make friends. I'm not going to eat that shit no matter how hungry I get.*

He slid the rifle under the truck and behind the tires where it was out of sight. It was getting very dark outside and he hoped he could find it again. *Maybe I should walk back out to the track and come back in so it would look like I was just walking down the track and not through the salvage yard.*

Teddy was proud of his quick thinking. Not something he was known for. He walked back and then started walking toward the hobos.

Thelma was extremely worried and wanted Jack to call the sheriff and report Teddy missing. They were still sitting at the supper table while the housekeeper gathered the dishes. "Jack you don't know. He could be lying out there somewhere not able to help himself". She dabbed at her eyes while she talked. The years had not been kind to Thelma but she tried her best to always look presentable and have a good face on. She went to the hairdresser three times a week and worked out at home in the gym Jack had set up for her. Her blonde hair had gone though several shades over the years and right now it was almost fake platinum. She had a few pounds she could lose but nothing to get that worked up about. All in all, she had done well with what she had to work with.

Thelma had discovered the missing money from her purse this morning when she was shopping but hadn't said anything to Jack. He would just make a big issue out of it.

Jack had taken a moment to digest what Thelma said to him and now he was ready with his response. "Thelma you know as well as I do, that little bastard is probably walking around Iowa City right now, looking for some flea bitten whore to bed down with, but he will be back as soon as he gets hungry enough. The only thing he can't live long without is food. Nope, I'm not going to call the Sheriff, and you know what? I am not going to worry about Teddy either. I have busted my ass for that kid and all he has done is make me mad and disappointed. He has never done one goddamn thing to make us proud of him."

Thelma started to sob and left the room, walking rapidly up the ornate winding staircase to her bedroom and closing the door. She flung herself down on the big bed and buried her head in the pillow finishing her cry. It wasn't just Teddy being gone that upset her, it was the way Jack treated her like a stupid kid that also upset her. Her and Jack had never had a decent discussion in all of the years they had been married. She had just done what Jack wanted and kept her mouth shut.

To say Teddy wasn't afraid would be incorrect, but at the same time he was cold and needed to know where he was at and those inconveniences trumped his fear. After all they were just a couple of hobos. What the hell could they do to him? He had brought along that can of spam as a little measure of friendship and something to break the ice but he was still watching them closely as he came up to the barrel.

The closest man to him looked up as he approached. He was dressed in an old navy pea jacket, the collar pulled up around his ears. He had a pair of holey sorrel boots on with no laces in them. His eyes looked tired with the flames from the fire reflecting in them. His long unkempt hair looked oily and curly. Otherwise he remained expressionless.

The other man did not acknowledge Teddy as he walked up with the can of spam extended in his right hand.

"Though you guys might like a bite to eat," Teddy said.

The man in the pea jacket grunted and took the can examining it as if he thought it might be some kind of a trick.

"I just got in here and I'm so damn cold, you don't mind if I warm up a bit do you?"

Nether man answered him as Teddy nervously extended his hands over the flames.

"Where you guys from?"

Teddy heard a whoosh behind him and managed to turn slightly before something came down on the back of his neck. His knees buckled and he fell against the barrel burning his hands as he slid down the side of it.

He was aware of them talking and going through his pockets and then the feeling in his extremities started to return. All he could think was to get away from them as fast a possible so he started crawling away from them and the barrel, on his hands and knees. His hands hurt so badly and things were being made worse by the glass and sharp objects he was crawling over. Teddy finally got to his feet and ran.

He ran about a hundred feet and then ducked behind an old bus to regain his senses. A quick look around the bus told him they were still standing by the barrel and now there were three of them.

Teddy reached for the back of his neck. There was a lump there but nothing felt broken or bleeding. *Why had those bastards hit him? He was only trying to be friends. He had brought them the can of spam.* Suddenly anger replaced his fear and he started looking for the truck body where he had hid the rifle. It was to his right about a hundred feet away. He would have to retreat deeper into the sea of junk cars and then make his way back to it.

I'll fix you, you son of a bitch. No one hits Teddy and takes his money and then just stands there, warming their dirty hands like nothing happened.

He made a wide circle peeking from behind the mountains of junk back in the direction of the burning barrel. They were busy laughing at their good fortune and eating the spam.

The truck body loomed in front of him and Teddy fell to his knees searching for the rifle behind the tires. His hands closed on the cold metal and he sat on the ground for a moment to decide what he was going to do next. He was starting to shiver again. He needed to do it quickly, before he was shaking too badly and would not be able to sight the rifle.

Teddy started walking toward them the rifle pulled tight into his shoulder. When he was about fifty feet away he hollered.

"All right you assholes. I want you to put my money back on the ground and start running before I blow you're ugly heads off."

The hobo in the coat stopped chewing his spam and looked back over his shoulder and then nudged the others who were paying little attention. They all turned and looked at him.

"You heard me put my money on the ground." He wasn't sure which one had it at this point so he waved the rifle at all of them. The third man, whom Teddy had not seen when he first approached them, and the one who had hit him, bent over and placed some bills on the ground. At least it looked like bills.

Teddy had stopped walking fearing they would rush him if he got to close.

"Now start walking away from here."

His finger on the trigger was freezing and the barrel of the gun was shaking. He could feel something wet running down his leg and he felt like he was going to throw up.

The men had still not moved, all three of them just standing there, hands out in front of them looking confused.

"What do you need a goddamn invitation," Teddy hissed at them. He was walking toward them again. Then he tripped and the gun went off.

He saw the dust come out of the man's jacket in the light of the fire, as the bullet tore through his shoulder and the hobo fell backwards into the barrel tipping it over and sending fire exploding out onto the ground. The other two men took off running into the darkness.

"Oh Jesus I didn't mean to do that." Teddy was getting to his feet again and now running toward the barrel and the fallen man. He stood over the moaning man for a moment, and then panicked and ran for the tracks.

He ran along side of the train stumbling in the rocks. The boxcars all looked the same in the dark but his was the one with the door partly opened. He flung the rifle in and hoisted his fat body in the door and just as quickly slid it shut.

It was completely dark but Teddy groped his way to the end of the car and the mound of cardboard that had been his refuge and crawled back under it.

He had never been so cold in his life and now he had pissed his pants to make things even worse. His burned hands felt like they were still on fire. He fumbled around in the dark and found his gym bag. Pulling off his overalls he changed his underwear.

Would they look for him? Would they call the cops? He lay there and listened quietly while all kinds of thoughts of what might happen flicked through his mind. Then the reality of it all hit him. *He had no money and very little food and water. He was thousands of miles from home and he had no idea where he was.* Teddy started crying.

CHAPTER FIVE

Thelma waited until just before supper and then called the sheriff. Jack would be home soon and he would never let her call if he was home, so if she was going to call, it was now or never.

The operator asked for her address and if it was an emergency. "Oh goodness no," Thelma replied, "No emergency but my son has been missing for a couple of days and I just wondered if the Sheriff had maybe seen him. He can get into mischief from time to time."

"How old is your son?" he asked.

"He's sixteen, but he is large for his age so you might think he was much older."

He took her name and address and explained that kids do run away, so he was sure there was nothing wrong but he would pass the information on to the patrol. If they had a car in the area, someone would stop by and talk to her but they were very busy right now.

Thelma hung up the phone and dabbed at her eyes. She wasn't so sure everything was all right anymore. She looked at the clock on the wall. Jack would be home soon so she better have something fixed for him to eat.

Teddy had heard footsteps outside in the rocks a few times, but the rest of the night was uneventful. He had settled down, when he warmed up a bit and then fallen to sleep. When he awoke he could see daylight, through the crack in the door.

He had gone back and forth in his mind, with leaving the boxcar or waiting and hoping the train took off again. If it was warmer outside he would have left. That and if he could have been sure, people out there were not looking for him. He could walk back to the rail yards and try to find another train but then again he might be seen. This train however could be sitting here for a long, long, time.

He had heard a lot of commotion back by the end of the train early this morning, and the sound of cattle bawling and men talking so maybe they were unloading them. They would have had to do something with them. It had been over a day since they had loaded them up back there and he knew they would need food and water.

Right now he had a worse problem and that was the fact he had to move his bowels. *He hated to do it in the boxcar with him living there but right now he just had no choice did he?*

Teddy walked to the far end of the car, passing the rifle that was still lying in the middle of the floor and his pair of wet shorts he had tossed out there. He reached down and picked the shorts up. They were a little dry and maybe he could use them to wipe his butt on. As soon as he had removed his overalls and bent over to assume the position the train lurched and Teddy reached for the wall to keep from falling backwards into his own mess. The train was backing out of where they were.

Pulling up his pants, as he ran to the door, he slid it open a bit and looked out. They were passing a stockyards and that was why they had come here. The sign on the building said, Denver Cattleman's Association. That answered two questions for him. Where he was and why they had come here. His only other question was, where in the hell was he going? He hoped it was back to Iowa.

The train went backwards until it cleared the siding and then stopped-- reversed directions and headed through the busy railroad yards. Teddy opened up the door a little more so he could see out of it and two things were evident. They were leaving Denver and from the direction of the sun, it looked like they were going south. The clickety clack of the wheels on the track increased in tempo until they were going faster than they had ever gone since Teddy got on the train. There was nothing to do but sit back and wait. He still had some water; one can of spam and some cookies. After that things could get tough.

For the rest of the day, and into the evening the train wailed its way past small towns and crossings. It seemed to be getting warmer and the mountains seemed to be falling farther and farther away. At least the high mountains, he had seen coming into Denver were. They were still in mountains, but they were more like rolling hills and the tracks curved around a lot of them. They crossed gorges on high trestles and for a long time ran parallel to a river. The scenery was beautiful. Now however it seemed like the terrain was becoming more and more desert like. At least Teddy assumed it was desert. He had never been in the desert.

Darkness came once more and Teddy ate the rest of his cookies. He just wasn't ready for the spam yet. His mood had lightened from this morning and his neck, which had been very sore this morning, was feeling a lot better. He just had a small lump back there and some new insight on trusting strangers.

That was not to say he wasn't worried. He was. He had no money and no plans, and that was not a good situation at all. He would worry about it when the train stopped, because this time he was getting off to stay.

Morton Valley did not have an organized Police Department, so the County Sheriffs Office, from the county, seat provided law and order from thirty miles away. Despite the distance there was rarely a time when a Deputy was not minutes off. Sheriff Clem Nash took good care of Morton's people.

The deputy who stopped to see Thelma came at the wrong time as Jack had just arrived home and was not in a good mood at all. He was eating when the man showed up, so Thelma answered the door.

The deputy who answered the call was a large man named Barney Carlson who had been a county sheriff's deputy and a permanent fixture around Morton for as long as most people could remember. Barney had an enormous belly and his wide black gun belt gun belt looked like it was stretched to its last notch and he carried more tools of the trade on it then a high line worker. His shirt was always stretched open a little showing you his hairy belly button.

He had one other disgusting habit that people always noticed, and that was he sweated profusely, even in the dead of winter. Today was no exception and he held his badly stained hat over his chest with one hand, while he wiped his leaking brow on his sleeve, breathing hard, apparently from the trip up the long front steps.

Thelma tried to talk quietly and not interrupt Jacks supper, but their voices carried all to well in the large foyer, and soon Jack was there all enraged and he barged right into their conversation.

"God damn it Thelma, I told you to not bother anyone with this. Hi Barney, she had no call to bother you with this. This is a family problem and really not a problem at all." He flashed Barney a thin forced smile and the fat deputy just looked at him a little bit bewildered with the whole charade.

Jack still had his white dinner napkin tucked in his pants and a piece of half eaten chicken in his right hand. "The damn kid is no good," Jack screamed at Barney. "If the fat little asshole decided to strike out on his own, then so be it. Just forget she ever called you," he told Barney, who now stood, looking completely confused and befuddled.

Thelma turned, fled from the room and up the curved stairs behind them. Totally embarrassed and equally defeated, she flung herself on the bed, pounding the pillow with her fists. How could this man hate his own son like this? How could he treat her like this?

The bedroom door flew open and Jack hurried across the room grabbing her by the wrists as she turned to look up at him. He held her up off the bed so he could talk to her face to face.

"I told you not to let this out Thelma. What part of that didn't you understand? I have an image to keep in this town, and Teddy does not embellish that image for either of us. For a long time he has made us look like fools in this town and I gave up on him a long time ago. The boy was a wasted effort Thelma and I should have jacked him in the toilet, instead of into you, the day he was conceived but it is too late for that, so you let go of this Thelma. If he's run off on his own, than good riddance." He screamed. "You let go of this or go and lie with your pig of a son. Do you understand" He flung her backwards on the bed, her head banging off the headboard.

She could only sob and hide her face in the pillows. She didn't want to cry in front of him

Downstairs, Barney the deputy, who was still standing in the front foyer, shook his head and closing the door behind him waddled down the sidewalk to his cruiser. *Just another couple of nut cases* he thought. He had too much to do without quacks like this, wasting his time and anyway it was suppertime and the sight of that chicken leg of Jacks had wet his appetite. He let go with a resounding fart and fanned his butt as he walked down the sidewalk. He didn't want that stink in his car.

The scenery had changed from rock covered mountains and scrubby pine trees, to desert and red rocks. There were no more lakes and rivers, just miles and miles of stubby trees and hard sand desert. Teddy sat in the doorway, smoking and flicking the cigarette butts in the brush to see if he could start a fire. His fat legs dangled out the doorway as he watched the world going by his eyes and hoped for some sign of civilization. The warm air felt good on his face and he was more relaxed now that he wasn't cold. He hoped the train would stop soon, so he could get off.

The next stop for the train was Santa Fe, New Mexico and it was only fifty miles down the track. They would be there in another hour. The conductor in the caboose had seen Teddy sitting in the boxcar and had every intention of tossing him off the train the minute they stopped.

In Santa Fe, Billy Joe Stanton sat on a bench outside of the Frontier Bar smoking one cigarette after another and staring at the railroad tracks across the street from him. He was feeling restless, but that was nothing new for him, he had always been restless.

Billy Joe was tall and lean, with a head of flaming red hair that he wore long, covered with a black Stetson hat, and he had a fiery a temper to go with the hair. He was always well groomed; keeping his hair combed and his face clean-shaven. He sported a mouth full of sparkling white teeth that he surrounded with a mischievous smile and sparkling blue eyes that looked almost wet.

Billy Joe was a smooth talker and had in the past talked many a woman into doing things she didn't want to do, and then made her regret it. The only thing he had failed to do was keep a woman. He had quit school in the eighth grade and bounced around from one worthless job to the next. He was fired more frequently than not, mostly for his belligerent attitude. Then when he was eighteen he ran away and joined the army. He did all right for a while as he had a natural fascination for guns and weapons and he won many medals and honors for marksmanship. Then about a year into his stint, his big mouth got the best of him and he told off and smacked his commanding officer. As Billy Joe's commanding officer said about him at his court martial. "He is one of the few people I ever met, who you had to learn to hate for your own damn good. That son of a bitch could sell sand to an Egyptian and make him believe he got a good deal."

Billy Joe came back to New Mexico and between run-ins with the law; he managed to eke out a living burglarizing houses and stealing cars. He liked to drink, whore around, and buy fancy clothes and that took a lot of money. More than he could make working at an honest job, but he was smart and rarely got caught in his fiendish deeds. He did need to expand his horizons however, as there just was not enough money in the petty things he had been doing. Today sitting here on this bench, he was planning a bigger job, but he needed someone to drive a getaway car. This would be his first attempt at robbing a business and he had no plans to get caught.

Teddy saw the buildings ahead as the train came out of the mountain pass and headed down the hill into Santa Fe. He retreated back to his cardboard and packed up his meager belongings. This was his stop, if the train stopped. The rifle still lay on the floor and he picked it up and ejected the spent shell he shot the hobo with and loaded a fresh one in the chamber. Hell this was the Wild West and no one would pay any attention to a man with a rifle. He was keeping it. He hoped the poor bastard he shot didn't die, but he was glad he evened the score and would not hesitate to do it again. People had been pissing him off for way too long.

The pile of his own excrement in the other corner had drawn some flies and for a second he aimed at it with the rifle. Maybe he would blow it all over the car in one last hurrah, but not until he was sure he was getting off. He drank the last of the water and flung the container out the door watching it bouncing along the desert floor before disappearing in the brush. The train jerked onto a siding and began slowing down rapidly and then stopped. Teddy had arrived.

When Billy Joe first saw Teddy walking towards him, his first impulse was to get up and go back inside the bar. But something about Teddy's confident swagger and that rifle in his hand told him this deserved another look.

"Hey you just get off that train," Billy Joe asked.

"Yeah. That ok with you?" Teddy was giving him his best glare, the rifle swung over his shoulder.

Billy laughed at Teddy's false bravado. "Where you going, and what the hell you doing carrying a rifle like that around." he asked? "Cops see you and you will be in the pokey fat boy."

Teddy looked over at the gun and then held it down along side his leg to make it look less conspicuous. Maybe he had found somebody here he could trust.

"I need something to eat and drink and I don't have any money. Some shithead bums back in"----.

Billy Joe waved his hand to tell him to shut up. "Give me the rifle kid and let's see what we can find you."

Teddy looked at the gun and then at Billy Joe. *Could he trust him, and did he have a choice?* He pushed the rifle at Billy Joe. "Watch out its loaded."

Billy looked the gun over. This was a Winchester model, 94, 30/30-lever action. They were a dime a dozen, but this one had a monogrammed stock and a shiny gold trigger. "Let's toss this in my truck and we can go inside and talk. How old are you kid?" He slapped Teddy on the back as they walked towards a red Chevy pickup parked in the lot.

It had been four days since Teddy had vanished and Thelma was grief stricken. She had cried until she was all cried out and then she had cried some more. Teddy was not all right and she could sense it.

Thelma and Jack had long gone to worship in the old brown church on the hill that had sat just in front of the town cemetery for over a hundred years. This was sacred ground where all of Jacks relatives were buried. The Morton section contained over forty head stones.

Over the years the churches denomination had changed from the original Baptist, to some kind of free evangelical church, and now just lately it had changed again. "It was now the Free Church of the Saints of Morton Valley," announced the new Pastor T.B Whistler.

This had been more than Jack could swallow and the day the announcement was made, he had stood and walked out dragging Thelma behind him. That had been a year ago and that decision was still fine with Jack. He'd rot in hell before he went back there.

Thelma however was frail and now the events of the last few days had driven her to the depths of despair and she needed help. Dressed in a black dress with white pearls and looking almost like she was in official mourning, she showed up on Pastor Whistler's doorstep.

T. B., the initials standing for Thurgood Barnabus, met her at the parsonage door in his pajamas at ten thirty in the morning. His grayer than black hair was sticking out in every direction, and his potbelly was hanging over his red pajamas bottoms. The fly in his drawers was open just enough that Thelma had caught a glimpse of something she had not seen for a long time, and surely did not want to see on this man of God. She raised her eyes to the ceiling.

"I need to talk to someone about my Son Teddy. He has disappeared and I am afraid he is in harms way." She was starting to cry again.

Pastor Whistler was excited that someone had actually come to pour their heart out to him. Business had not been that good and he was feeling neglected. The jubilant Pastor asked Thelma to walk over to the church and wait for him and he would be right over. He rushed back into the house to put on his clerical garb, leaving Thelma on the porch.

For a second, Thelma thought about just walking away and not looking back. Maybe Jack had been right about this weird little fat man and his new church. Before she could formulate a good decision however, Pastor Whistler was out the front door and taking her hand with his right hand while he pulled up his suspenders with his left, they were on the way to the side door of the church across the yard.

The church was dark and cold but the little room in the front that was the pastor's study was in stark contrast to the rest of the building. It had a large stained glass window with bright sunlight streaming in and an old oil burner in the corner was percolated heat throughout the room. The room was littered with books and piles of papers stacked everywhere. On the desk was an old porcelain coffee cup with what looked like used motor oil in it.

Thelma was directed to a black leather chair in front of the pastor's desk and he took a matching one right beside her, still holding her right hand in his chubby hand.

"Now tell me about Teddy." He said looking very concerned. He was now patting her right hand softly while he held it with his left hand.

"Well Theodore-- Teddy I mean-- and his father have never gotten along. You see Teddy is a spirited child who has been picked on all of his life." She dabbed at her eyes with her lace handkerchief. "I really shouldn't be wasting you time" she said.

"No-No," Pastor Whistler almost shouting, gripping her hand tighter and scooting his chair closer. "That's what I am here for. You have come seeking help my child and I am that beacon of light you need so badly." He leaned forward almost nose to nose to emphasis his point. The smell of onions, garlic and whiskey on his breath hit Thelma like exhaust out of a hot tail pipe, and she winced, turning her head to the side.

The portly pastor sensed he was repulsing her and backed off dropping her hand and settling back into his chair smiling.

Thelma quickly retrieved her hand and hid it in her lap under her purse. *She had made a big mistake coming here. This man was weird. How many ministers would show up at the front door looking like he did, in his pajamas with his genitals peeking out. He was disheveled and stunk. She had to leave and now.* Her eyes were darting around the room looking for another door.

"I need to use the bathroom," she said. "I think I'm going to be ill."

"Certainly," he smiled. "It's right down those stairs and to the left." He pointed to another door directly across from the one they had entered.

When Thelma reached the bottom of the stairs she kept right on walking past the bathroom doors, through a kitchen, and out another door in the back of the church. She broke into a panicked run through the cemetery, her black skirts and white petticoats, flashing like the checkered flag at the Indy five hundred. By the time T.B. Whistler realized she was not coming back, she was out of sight and he was out of luck

At the bank, Jack Morton reclined behind his desk in his over stuffed swivel chair. His right leg propped on top of the desk, his head was tilted back as he enjoyed his first cigar of the day. He was feeling especially pompous and a wee bit arrogant today. His fight with Thelma last night had only fortified his hate for Teddy. *Why, when things were going so good, did that fat ass have to try and ruin everything?*

His son Jack Jr. was sitting across from him dreaming of the day he would be on that side of the desk. He emulated his father in everything except the cigars. They made him sick to his stomach.

"I called you in here son to let you know that your little brother may have left us for greener pastures. He's been gone four days and it's never been so peaceful except for your mothers over reaction to things. I was wondering if you might stop by the house today and cheer her up a little. Bring the grandkids and the little woman along."

"No idea where he went?" Jack Jr. had a smile and a quizzical look to him.

"NO! He screamed. I don't give a rat's ass where he went either. Out of sight out of mind." He took another big drag on his cigar.

Jack Jr. chuckled. He hated his brother almost as much as his father. Sure dad. I can do that for Mother. He stood up and straightened the seam in his pants. I'll call Marylyn and set it up for tonight.

CHAPTER SIX

Teddy looked over at Billy Joe as they bounced across the desert, a large cloud of dust drifting off behind them. He was still a little suspicious about where he was going, but Billy seemed to be quite personable, and wanting to help him. "Beggars couldn't be that choosy," his Mom had said many times-- or something like that.

Mom. -- She had to be worried sick about him. But if he called her she would know he was ok, and tell his father, and he wanted his father to think he was dead or even worse off, if that was possible. Serve the asshole right. Maybe he could send her a note when he got some money. The truck skidded to a stop in front of an old dented up silver Air Stream trailer.

"Home sweet home kid. Grab your shit out of the back and come on in." Billy flashed one of his toothy smiles. Teddy reached for the rifle behind the seat.

"I'll bring that boy. You just bring yourself and the rest of your stuff." The smile had faded and he looked quite serious.

Teddy stayed, sitting outside at an old picnic table while Billy Joe took his rifle and went in the trailer. Teddy had no idea where he was. There was nobody else in sight and you could see a long way in the flat, almost nude, desert. Billy's place looked like a junkyard, with another old vehicle that had no wheels, lying on its side, the paint burned off by the desert sun. There were broken down appliances, mounds of rotting garbage and old windows and doors stacked everywhere. Also lots of beer bottles and oil cans littering the area.

The screen door banged and Billy Joe reappeared with a six-pack of beer. He opened one with an old rusty church key he fished out of his back pocket and drank about half of it, belched and pushed the opener and the pack at Teddy. "Here kid, have a beer. You'll feel better."

One beer led to another and one six-pack to another and all too soon Teddy was drunk. The hot desert sun was making him sweat a lot and soon he became dizzy and dizzier and threw up on the ground behind him.

Billy looked annoyed. "You all better go inside and rest a little bit buddy. Shame on you wasting all of that good beer like that." Billy came around the table and helped him into the trailer laying him down on a couch where he soon passed out.

When Teddy woke up and looked out the window, the sun was lower in the sky, but it was stifling hot in the trailer and his clothes were wet with sweat. He stared at the wood paneled ceiling still feeling dizzy and disoriented. The acid taste of puke in his mouth was still there.

The walls and ceiling were covered with pictures of naked girls from magazines, and Teddy's gaze went from one to the next. He had never seen pictures like this. At the far end of the trailer was a glossy black and white picture that was not out of any magazine. Teddy stood up and walked closer to see it better. It appeared to be a young Mexican girl lying on her back, her legs flung wide apart. There was nothing left to the imagination. Her breasts were small and virtually nonexistent. Teddy wasn't looking at her breasts however, he was only interested in what was between her legs and right now his face was no more than six inches from the picture. So finally, that was what one of them looked like.

He became aroused, as his anatomy was always one step ahead of his brain

He put his hand in his pocket to hide his excitement when the screen door slammed and Billy Joe let out a war hoop.

"Well lookey here. Our little boy done got himself all excited looking at old Billy Joe's girl friend. Shame on you Teddy. Get your hand out of your pocket before you have an accident." He laughed out loud at himself.

Teddy was completely embarrassed and he went from erect to flaccid in about a moment while stumbling back, and sitting down on the busted down couch.

Billy sensed his embarrassment and not wanting to make it any worse changed the subject.

"You know there is a river about a mile off boy and you need to clean up, cause you stink. You stink really bad. Once you get cleaned up, then we can go to town, and I will get you something to eat. Some of that really good Mexican food that you will really like." He seemed to have forgotten for the moment about Teddy's carnal desires.

The walk to the river cleared Teddy's head and by the time they got there he was feeling better and wasn't horny anymore. He stood by the bank looking at the water flowing by. It was a not a wide river, but an exceptionally clean river. The water appeared to be a few feet deep, flowing gently over a white sand bottom. It did look inviting.

Teddy heard footsteps behind him and when he turned around, here came Billy Joe naked as a jaybird. Teddy had never seen a mature man before naked. He was embarrassed to take his clothes off after seeing what Billy possessed, so he went down stream a ways, stripped and got in before Billy could see him. The water felt so good. Two days ago he had been freezing to death and now he was sweating in the desert. He washed out his underpants and hung them on a branch to dry in the breeze that had come up. That Mexican food Billy had talked about was going to taste pretty good. He was starved.

When Jack got home that night Thelma was no where to be seen. He ran upstairs and down calling for her. He thought, *I should have called and told her Jack Jr. and his family was coming over but it had slipped his mind. Hell, she never went anywhere.* Now he stood in the kitchen totally exasperated. *How could she do this to him?*

Jack reached for the phone on the wall. *Maybe she had run over to her mothers. They visited a lot.* Then he saw the note.

Jack, I can't just sit here any longer pretending everything is alright with Teddy. I have gone to Iowa City to look for him. I will call if I find out anything. I took the bus so don't worry.

Love Thelma

Jack tore up the note in a fit of rage. "Damn bitch." He screamed. Then he picked up the phone and called his son telling him not to come over.

Mama Maria's was not a posh restaurant by any standards. But it did serve a great Mexican cuisine and Billy Joe had long been a regular there for some time. The place looked like an old hacienda from the road, with its yellow stucco walls and red tile roof. Inside however, it was varnished wood paneling and white acoustical ceiling tiles that had turned yellow, with age and cigarette smoke. Red vinyl booths lined the windowed walls except for one corner, where there was a small stage. A tambourine and two drums sat unattended in front of a crooked microphone stand.

In the middle of the floor was a round bar, with swivel stools around the perimeter, all of them filled with people drinking and socializing. A temporary sign right inside the door scribbled on some cardboard, said, **Seat yourself.**

Billy Joe led the way in and he and Teddy slid into one of the booths. They had ridden in, in silence. Partly because of the noise of Billy Joe's truck missing its muffler but also because they still were still not that comfortable with each other. They had talked a little this afternoon. Billy Joe now knew Teddy wasn't eighteen as Teddy had lied to him. He also knew he had left home because he hated his Father, and had ridden a freight train across the country from Iowa.

"You know kid I have a business and I need a partner and I'm prepared to make you an offer if you are interested."

Teddy looked up at Billy. He nodded his head yes but said nothing.

Just then a young Mexican girl in a white frock and colorful skirts approached the table and asked, "Would you like to order Billy."

Teddy rung his hands and gave her his toothiest smile. "Bring us each a platter of enchiladas beautiful and a pitcher of beer. For me of course." he added. "He'll have a coke." He pointed at Teddy.

Teddy could only stare at her. She looked remarkably like the girl in the picture on the trailer wall. He could feel the blood rushing to his loins.

"As I was saying kid, I want to offer you a business proposition. You can stay with me for as long as you like and I will give you one fourth of everything we make. After taxes," he added and then slapped the table top laughing. "Just kidding about the taxes kid. Oh my God that was funny."

Teddy smiled at Billy Joe's humor attempt. "What kind of job is it?"

"It's not hard kid and you can do it easy."

"What kind of job is it," Teddy asked again?

35

Just then the girl was back with their food and drinks. "Extra big enchilada's tonight Billy. You're going to like them."

Billy reached out and touched her arm. "Not like I like your little Taco sweetheart."

She giggled and set their food down. She smelled like some kind of flowers to Teddy who was completely mesmerized by her. He was glad he was sitting down with a table top over his lap.

Billy had still not answered Teddy's question but he said, "Let's eat kid while it's hot. We can talk more on the way home and after I get you some new duds. You can't walk around looking like the farmer in the dell. This is western country Teddy, and as big as your ass is, they got jeans here to fit it." He poked Teddy in the overall pocket with his fork and laughed some more.

They ate and then went to a clothing store and Teddy walked out with new jeans, black cowboy boots and a white western style shirt. Teddy had stolen a look in the mirror in the store and he had to admit, he thought he looked pretty damn good. Maybe he and Billy Joe were meant to be partners. Just then his heel caught on the rough planks outside of the store and he fell against the railing much to Billy Joe's amusement.

"You walk like my little sister in her mommas high heels Teddy." Teddy laughed with him as he hoisted himself back up.

"You'll get used to them partner. You'll get used to them."

'Partner.' Teddy liked the sound of the word. No one had ever been his partner before. They headed back out of town in the noisy pickup with the windows cranked down, laughing, smoking cigarettes, and trading Mexican food farts in the cool desert air.

Thelma sat on a bus bench bewildered and uneasy. She had been on edge since The Reverend T.B. Whistler had flashed himself at her this morning. Iowa City was a big town and she had not made a dent in it and her feet were killing her. Maybe she should get a hotel room for the night and call it a day. She had flagged down a patrol car and showed them a picture of Teddy, asking if they would call her if they saw him. Both officers looked concerned, until Thelma was behind them. and then they burst out laughing.

"If I had a kid looked like that I would have given him money to leave home," the driver laughed. The other officer smiled and threw the picture on the dashboard. It had been a long night and he couldn't wait to get home.

Billy Joe sat down in the small booth that served as an indoor eating area in the small trailer and indicated to Teddy, to sit across from him. It was time for a serious talk.

A small gas light hissed away on the wall and served to give the place some heat in the cold desert night. He opened two bottles of beer and threw the key on the table top pushing one over to Teddy, who looked like a twelve year old waiting for the sex talk from his father.

"Before we start to talk kid, I want to know where you got the rifle." Billy was staring at Teddy, make him feel uncomfortable.

"It's mine, my Dad bought it for me."

Billy slid out of the booth and went outside coming back in with the gun and pointed it at Teddy.

"Unless your name is Frank Fields and you come from Wheaten Nebraska your fibbing to me Teddy." He swung the gun around showing him the brass plate bolted to the butt plate.

"Billy Joe sat back down after throwing the rifle down on the couch. "If you and me are going to be partner's kid, we have to be honest with each other. I'm going to give you one more chance before I throw your ass outside with the coyotes."

Teddy had screwed up and he knew it. He had no choice but too cooperate with Billy Joe.

"Sorry," he said. "I stole it out of a pickup."

"You shot it. Two shells are missing out of that magazine. No one half fills a magazine."

"I shot it once on the train in the box car," and then his voice trailing off he said, "I shot a bum."

"You shot what?" Billy screamed.

"A hobo who had hit me over the head and stole all of my money." He was now looking eye to eye with Billy Joe and looking dead serious.

37

Slowly a wide grin came over Billy Joes face. "Gawd damn it kid. You shot someone. Will I'll be damned. I got me a natural born killer here. That calls for another round of beer."

Billy slid two more beer across the table top but this time Teddy declined. He had a bad gut right now.

Billy put one beer back in the fridge and looked at Teddy with a smirk on his face. "You kill him kid?"

"Don't know. Never went back to look."

"You and I are going places kid." Billy was bubbling over with enthusiasm now. He laid out the whole plan for them and announced they were going to pull their first job day after tomorrow because he was broke.

Later, lying in the dark, wide awake with a terrible case of the jitters, Teddy could only bite his lip and wonder what in the hell had he got himself into. He could hear the coyotes that Billy had threatened him with, rummaging around in the garbage outside. The gaslight still hissed on the wall behind him casting a faint glow in the trailer. Billy had retired to the bedroom in the back of the trailer. It was the only room he had not been allowed in, or even allowed to look in. Billy kept it locked all the time. There was a small bathroom inside but you were only allowed to pee in it. If you had anything else to do Billy had dug a latrine outside.

A playboy centerfold of a young blond with huge breasts was staring down at him from the ceiling and it had the effect of ignited his simmering lust again. Looking for something more sensuous Teddy turned so he could see his favorite photo. That glossy picture at the end of the trailer. That was the filthiest picture he had ever seen and that girl in the restaurant tonight had looked so much like her, it had to be her. The picture was gone.

CHAPTER SEVEN

The next morning, bright and early, Billy Joe and his new partner practiced their tactics but first Billy had a little staff meeting at the picnic table. He had a Smith and Wesson thirty-eight-caliber revolver with an eight-inch barrel. The convincer he called it. It was a formable weapon indeed and he pointed it right at Teddy's forehead while he talked. "I don't want to shoot anyone kid but if you're going to talk the talk, you better look like you mean it. If you're not scaring them shitless, than you hasn't done your job." He smiled that big white toothy grin. He had shed his western clothes for a pair of old military greens.

"Now here's the way it's going to go kid, so listen up."

Teddy was still looking wide-eyed at the business end of that revolver but he nodded his head slowly in the affirmative.

"You know how to drive that truck right?" Billy waved the pistol in the direction of the old red pickup.

"Sure I drove trucks all the time out at my brother's farm." Teddy tried to look convincing but he wasn't that sure Billy was buying it.

"Well tomorrow morning kid you are going to be my getaway driver. You are going to park where they can't see you, and after I pull off the job, I'm going to come running out and you will pull up and let me in. Then we need to get the hell out of there."

"Who we going to rob?" Teddy asked.

"Well since it's our first job were gonna start small kid, so were gonna rob a gas station right here on the edge of town." Billy was leaning over the table almost face to face with Teddy, as if he had to talk low in case someone was listening. Teddy looked around but there was nothing but sage brush, sand and the usual junk.

"I've been at this station before and there is just one guy on duty in the mornings and he is usually working on cars in the back room. He runs out every time someone runs over that dinger hose to pump their gas, and he always keeps all of his money in his shirt pocket. You park in back of the station and I'll walk around and stomp on that damn hose, and when he comes walking out, I'll put this baby between his eyes and get the money." He picked the pistol up again and waved it in the air. "All you got to do is sit on your fat ass and wait for me understand?"

Teddy nodded his head.

Later that day Billy had Teddy drive the truck around the desert for a while until he was convinced he could do what he was supposed to do. Then they came back to the trailer and parked. Before Teddy could get out of the truck however, Billy made one other point.

"You wear those baggy ass overalls tomorrow that I found you in kid. You need to save those there clothes for good. Eaten out and shit like that."

"Speaking of eating Billy, I'm damn hungry." Teddy was afraid to say much, but this one complaint he had to get out. He moved closer to the door in case Billy was going to smack him. They had been eating only once a day when they went to town and that was just not enough for Teddy.

"You need to lose some of that fat kid. Need to look lean and mean like old Billy here." He thumped his own chest with his forefinger.

Teddy didn't press the issue. He could stand to lose a few pounds.

Thelma stayed in a fourteen dollar a night motel that night in Iowa City, but not before she called Jack and told him she was alright.

"Thelma you get your ass home," Jack ranted. "You ain't going to find him. When he gets good and hungry he'll come home like I told you. Bunch of no good foolishness that's what it is. If I wasn't so damn mad I would come and get you, but maybe a night away from each other will do us both a world of good."

"Jack I'm sorry," Thelma sobbed, "but Teddy is our son and how you can turn your back on him like this, is beyond me."

"Oh damn it Thelma grow up will you." Jack slammed the phone down. *Maybe he would go down to Casey's for a bite to eat and a few drinks. Maybe he could find someone to talk too who would understand how he felt. It was a cinch his dingbat wife didn't.*

Billy Joe and Teddy ate supper that night at the A&W drive in. Billy only had three bucks to his name. They ate in silence in the truck and then drove home to wait for the big day. That night Billy was all charged up. This was the start of something big. He could just feel it.

Out on the couch Teddy was also wide awake but not because he was charged up. He was so nervous he got sick to his stomach, and he went outside and puked up his papa burger. He missed his Mother and wished he could talk to her.

The day dawned clear as a bell. "A great day for a stickup," Billy said. He had heard Teddy retching outside last night and it bothered him that he was so nervous. *Better not chicken out*, he said to himself.

Billy drove in because he knew where the gas station was and parked the truck across the street and behind the station. "Now keep that engine going and keep you eyes pealed for cops. If you see cops you blow the horn you understand?"

Teddy shook his head yes. He felt like throwing up again, but swallowed hard to chase away the urge. His eyes flickered from one window to the next and from one mirror to the other looking for anything suspicious. *What in the hell had he got himself into? He could go to jail for a long time and then his father would have something to really blow steam off over. If he had any brains at all, and his father thought he didn't, he would get out of this truck and start walking right now.*

Then before he could think again Billy came running around the side of the station. His hand with the revolver was stuck in his shirt and his other hand was gripping a wad of money.

GO Kid!-- Billy was screaming and laughing all at the same time. He was pounding the dash and shouting," right" or "left" each time they came to an intersection.

Teddy careened around one corner at the last second and went way over on the other side of the street, forcing an old man on a bike way up on the sidewalk. The truck with no muffler was bellowing like a bear with his foot in a trap, but they kept flying down the road and out of town.

"It was too easy kid. Way to damn easy. I didn't have to stomp on that wire or nothing. That idiot was coming out of the garage with a bucket of water, and when he saw that gun he started crying like a baby and pleading for his life. I just grabbed his money and left."

Billy let out another war hoop as they left the road heading across the desert in a cloud of dust.

That afternoon Billy gave Teddy ten dollars and said that was his share plus payback for the money Teddy owed him.

"How much you get from the robbery?" Teddy asked.

"Sixty seven dollars my little fat friend. Sixty-seven dollars of the easiest money I ever made. Here, have a beer and then we can go down to the river and clean up. You probably got a shit spot in your shorts that need washing out." He laughed and uncapped two beers.

For the rest of April and May they continued on their crime spree. They hit a few more gas stations, a dry cleaner, and a shoe repair shop. They made as little as twenty dollars and as much as three hundred and fifty. They had no pattern, when they ran out of money; they went out and robbed someone.

Teddy was getting to be a seasoned robber and he was no longer as nervous as he was before their jobs. He didn't miss home as much as he used to either, and although he still missed his Mom a lot he still hadn't got the courage to call her. Hell they didn't even have electricity in the trailer, let alone a phone. Anytime they were in town, where there was a phone, he was with Billy, and he didn't want Billy to know he was needing his Mom like that and feeling sorry for what she must be going through.

Billy Joe however was getting restless and thinking about moving to Tucumcari. They were getting to be a hot item around Santa Fe in the newspapers and it was time to scat before they got caught. The last job they pulled, a good description of Billy's truck was shown on the news and Billy had seen the article the next night at Mama Maria's while they ate supper.

So one moment, on the tenth of June, Billy announced they were leaving next week for new territory. Teddy was lying on his busted down couch staring at the centerfold overhead again and wondering how it would feel to just put one of those breasts in his mouth like a nursing baby. For a few moments Teddy had no reaction to Billy Joe's announcement. Then he slowly sat up his hands in his lap, staring at the floor. He looked despondent and withdrawn and Billy could sense something was wrong.

"What's the matter kid? You got the blues or something?" Billy walked over and good naturedly ruffled Teddy's hair.

"You know you lost a lot of weight kid and it shows. You ain't got all of those damn zits all over your face anymore either. Looks good on ya kid. Must be clean living huh?"

Teddy smiled a little forced grin. He was well aware that he had changed and his diet change must have had something to do with it. All of that Mexican food that Billy liked, but come to think of it he had never seen a fat Mexican.

"Tomorrows my birthday," he muttered.

Billy sat down beside him. "No shit kid your big seventeen huh"

"Sixteen," Billy answered.

"Hey! You told me you were sixteen when we met. You lying to me again kid."

"No. I said that before you told me never to lie to you again. Guess I'm just setting the record straight."

Things were quiet for a time. Teddy just sat there thinking and Billy lit a cigarette and played with the transistor radio trying to get better reception. Patsy Cline was pouring out her heart singing "Crazy" and Billy loved that song. He was crazy too, but for a different reason than Patsy.

Billy finally broke into a big grin, walked over and slapped Teddy on the back. "You got balls kid. I like that and you know what tomorrow night you and me are going to have a going away party, and a birthday party just for you. I'm going to get us some women."

Teddy ears perked up and he looked at Billy with a surprised look on his face.

"Women?"

"Yea kid, women, with hot pants for you and me."

Teddy was all smiles now too. Maybe he was going to finally get laid.

"You ever been with a woman kid?"

Teddy still grinning said "No but I want to."

"Man can't just want to Teddy, he has to. You know what happens when you play with yourself?"

Teddy was getting red in the face but he shook his head yes. He didn't like acknowledging that first he was a virgin, and second that he had played with himself.

"Well you have to get rid of that stuff from time to time kid. Now I knows you can do that by yourself but that's not really getting rid of it kid, that's just letting the pressure off. Kind of like when the beer bottle fizzes when you pop the cap. It takes a woman to get it all out of there. Yep. Clean as a whistle your little sack will be."

Teddy was listing intently and grinning broadly. Billy Joe had a way with words.

Billy had sat back down beside Teddy once more. He lit two cigarettes and gave one to Teddy. "You know kid, when I was in the army. I knew this guy from Oklahoma City named Clete. Old Clete he was just like a doctor being a medic and all. Clete told me that if you get too many sperms in your system it can back up your spinal cord and get into your brain fluid and drive you crazier than a hyena. I reckon that was reason enough for me to keep the pump working, and just look at me kid. I'm as smart as they come kid. Ain't that for sure."

Teddy knew that Billy liked to spin yarns, but this time maybe there was something to what he said. *Maybe that's what happened to my Father.* He thought, *I bet his brain is swimming in sperm, he thought.*

Thelma was an emotional wreck. She had come home from Iowa City totally defeated. Jack had met her at the door with a smirk instead of a smile. Thelma really believed he was out of his mind with his pompous attitude and his righteous indignation.

As the days ticked into weeks she became more and more withdrawn and depressed. She no longer believed Teddy was alive and she hoped that someone would find his body so she could bring him home to that little cemetery on the hill that she fled through a while back. She knew one thing, if that happened she would pay for a Preacher to come from another town and perform the service. She had had a vision of T.B. Whistler standing over her sons casket with his pants unzipped.

Thelma had few friends, and the ones she did have, preferred to not be around her when she was in the funk she was in. Jack had all but abandoned her, sleeping in the guest room and staying out late at night with his friends and business acquaintances.

In his heart he too sensed something was wrong and yes there was a part of him that mourned the loss of his son. But it was all for the best he reasoned.

The next day Billy Joe and Teddy went to the river one last time to clean up for the party tonight. Teddy was no longer self-couscous about being with Billy naked since he had lost all of the weight, and they walked into the water side by side. Maybe he didn't match up with Billy anatomically but he was getting there and he was only sixteen. Beside's tonight he was going to come of age.

After they walked back to the trailer they sat, drank beer and smoked cigarettes until suppertime. Billy reminded Teddy to have his bags packed as they were leaving at dawn's first light tomorrow. Billy also said that tonight he would be going into town alone to pick up the women and he would bring Teddy back something to eat. He had some unfinished business he needed to take care of and he didn't want Teddy with him. So about five p.m Billy left Teddy at the picnic table and disappeared in a cloud of dust.

It was hot in the sun so Teddy retreated back to the confines of the trailer to wait. He was nervous about meeting a girl in a romantic encounter for the first time. How many times had he'd fantasized about this moment and now it was almost here. He walked to the bathroom to look in the mirror and make sure he was looking his best, trying the door to Billy's bedroom as he passed it. It was still locked as it had been all of the other times he had checked. What was in there that was such a secret?

He studied his face in the mirror. He had changed radically in the last two months. Maybe people wouldn't think he was such an ugly lard ass now.

Teddy packed all of his belonging in his old red gym bag and it was stuffed. He would leave all of his old fat clothes here. He was never going to be like that again. He lay down and looked at the girl on the ceiling again. Yea, his pump was primed and he was ready. He was tired and fell asleep.

Maybe it was the sound of a vehicle approaching, and maybe it was the war hoop Billy Joe let out as they slid to a stop in a cloud of dust but Teddy was jolted awake. It was Billy all right with two women but where the hell was the old red truck. They were in a white Mercury convertible with a set of long horn steer horns bolted to the hood.

"Get your ass out here Teddy I got us some poontang." Billy was standing on the front seat and the women where having hysterics over his antics. Her jumped over the door opened the trunk and came out with a case of beer and handed it to Teddy.

"Let's get inside kid and get this party going." He shoved a lit cigar in Teddy's open mouth as he passed him.

The two women stepped out of the car and followed Billy inside. One of the girls was about Teddy's age he guessed, and the other looked like she was about ten years older. They both had colorful dresses on and wore little makeup, except for gold hoop earrings. Their hair was in identical ponytails that bobbed up and down as they walked.

Teddy could not take his eyes off the younger girl hanging on Billy's arm. She had to be the girl in the glossy photo. He had only seen her picture that one time, but then, he hadn't spent a lot of time looking at her face. If only he could see her bottom half, then he would know for sure.

Teddy, who was grinning with anticipation, was saying nothing as he quietly followed the trio inside. Billy was already sitting down in the booth and kissing the younger girl who was responding by looking like she was eating his face.

"Teddy this is Carman" Billy said introducing the girl who was now trying to shove her tongue in his ear.

Billy laughingly pushed her away and then pointing to the older girl who up to now had been relatively inactive he said. "This is Deloris and she will be yours for the night."

Billy could not believe what he had heard. He didn't want Deloris he wanted Carman. Carman, the girl from the glossy picture that he'd been fantasizing over for two months. Carman who in that inviting sexually suggested pose had said I want you Teddy. Carman who now had her head under the table, doing God knows what in Billy's lap.

Before he could protest however Billy Joe and Carman slipped out of the booth and were gone into Billy's bedroom.

Deloris snapped her gum and looking over at Teddy said. "Shy kid. Maybe this will get the ball rolling. She had turned partially sideways on the seat and pulled one leg up revealing that there were no panties under that dress. "That's the place all men want to go back to kid." She pointed between her legs.

Teddy could only stare at her his mouth hanging open. "Pet it kid. It won't bite you," she said, opening her legs wider.

By this time Teddy was so ready he couldn't think straight. In fact the only thing that was straight was his anatomy and all of his inhibitions had disappeared like a bolt of lightning. His brain was fogged over with sperm and a severe lack of blood. She was unbuckling his pants as his trembling hand was fondled her.

"Well lookie here" she said digging in Teddy's pants. His hand on hers and her massaging him was all that it took. Teddy moaned he could wait no longer.

Deloris screamed and laughed in delight. While Teddy gathered himself together and bolted out the door into the cool desert night.

Teddy was totally humiliated and that was putting it mildly. What had been promised to be his coming of age, his deflowering, had tuned into a total failure. He was no man. He was just a horny little kid who was destined to someday have his brain saturated with seminal fluid.

Teddy didn't get far in the desert before his fear of the coyotes and the unknown had kicked in, so he made his way back to the only refuge he had. The unoccupied car. He slid inside and laid down on the front seat. The keys were in it hanging from the ignition just inches from his eyes. He could just drive away and not look back, nothing was stopping him. He had almost three hundred dollars in his billfold and that would be enough to get him back to Iowa and his Mother if he could find his way. The thought of escape was there, but there was also another stronger thought about Billy Joe. Billy was the first person in his life that had paid attention to him. The first person who made him feel needed, that is except his mother but that didn't count. Mother's had to love their kids no matter how ugly and screwed up they were. But him and Billy, they were partners, and partners just didn't do that. He crawled in the back seat and went to sleep.

When he awoke it was the middle of the night and he had to pee. Teddy slipped outside the car and when he was finished with his call to nature, he crept up to the trailer and peeked in the door. Deloris was nowhere to be seen. The old dilapidated couch was empty, his red gym bag beside it right where he had left it. He stretched his neck farther holding the door open, but still standing outside. The door to Billy's bedroom was open.

Teddy stepped inside as softly as he could and peered in Billy's room. He had never looked in there before, and the only light was coming from a faint gaslight flickering in the corner of the bedroom. Billy was asleep on his back, one girl on each side of him. Their legs were flung over him like they were holding him down and hiding his nakedness. Their heads were touching on his chest, both of them fast asleep. They were all naked but Teddy was not feeling anything sensual about the scene. It was just a bunch of bare asses. They just looked so peaceful. He lay back down on the couch and drifted back to sleep.

"Come on kid get your ass up were hitting the road." Billy was standing over him a cigarette hanging from his mouth as he talked.

"Where are the girls?" Teddy asked while rubbing his eyes.

"I took them home an hour ago kid. Hey, Deloris said she had a good time with you."

"She did?" Teddy said.

"Yep and that girl never lies. Let's get this show on the road."

The trunk was loaded with all of Billy's stuff and the rifle so Teddy threw his bag in the back seat. Then Billy, with a can of gasoline, set fire to the trailer.

"Where did you get this?" Teddy asked. Gesturing to the car they were sitting in.

Let's just say I got a hell of a deal kid. He hit the gas and they were gone in a cloud of dust.

CHAPTER EIGHT

Thelma had decided she couldn't take sitting around bawling over Teddy any longer. She had to do something. She had found a sympathetic ear in her son Clyde and his wife Sharon.

Clyde and Teddy were the closest in age of the four kids, even though there was still over ten years between them. They had lived together for a few years and they did have one thing in common. They both hated Jack, although it was with different degrees of intensity. Clyde was content to just stay away from the old man and mind his own business. He lived on a farm and seldom came to town, letting Sharon take care of all of the business in town.

Sharon never came to town without stopping to see her mother-in-law, so over the years they had developed a reasonable relationship. Sharon didn't like Teddy but she kept it to herself, and she and Clyde were aware he had been missing.

Thelma rarely mentioned Teddy when they talked. She sensed Sharon's feelings for her youngest son and she was not naive. She knew that was one subject better left alone.

So on that Monday morning the first day of July, when Sharon came to town and, picked up Thelma for lunch, they went downtown to Irma's, a trendy café. At least for Morton Valley it was trendy. It had white tablecloths and waitresses dressed in black skirts and frilly blouses. There were no hamburgers on the menu and your water always had a slice of lemon in it. They had their own clientele and it did appear that there were enough of them, to keep things on the right side of the ledger board.

"I will be glad next year when the last kid is in school so I have more time to do things. We need to get out like this more often." Sharon took a drink of her water and waited for a reply, the ice still tinkling in her glass.

Thelma had been unusually quiet today. They had ridden from her house to the café in silence, except for when Sharon had asked her where they should go.

Thelma had replied with one word, "Irma's." Now she smiled softly and talked so low that Sharon could hardly hear her. "It's hard to believe that little one is that old already."

"I know, Clyde and I can hardly believe it ourselves."

The waitress came and took their orders. Thelma ordered a salad and Sharon had a chicken sandwich.

Thelma had a piece of the white linen table cloth between her fingers, and she was feeling of it between her finger and thumb, as if she was checking the thread count, her eyes lowered to her lap. She was dressed as always, impeccably in a blue skirt and a plain white blouse. She had a single strand of pearls around her neck and a solitary pearl in each ear ring.

"Sharon, does Clyde have any opinions or comments about Teddy's disappearance, or don't you talk about it?" Thelma was looking at her with tears in her eyes. Sharon knew the subject would come up. She didn't think it would be the first thing on the agenda though.

Sharon wore her hair cut short in a pixie cut and she ran her fingers through it as if she was searching for the right words. Unlike Thelma, she was dressed in jeans and colorful print blouse. She wore no jewelry or make up.

"I know he's concerned but you know Clyde, he doesn't like to get involved in other people business."

"His own brother missing is other peoples business?" Thelma had a scowl on her face that made Sharon feel very uncomfortable.

"Well you know what I mean," Sharon said trying to keep things light. Teddy and he are not that close. My God Thelma, there is almost ten years between them. Teddy was still a young boy when Clyde left home, and yes I know Teddy has worked out on the farm a couple of times, but Clyde said it was more trouble than it was worth."

It was not the answer Thelma had wanted, but before she could say anything else their orders came. They ate in silence for a few minutes before Thelma spoke, a little louder than last time.

Sharon could see the tears that were not that far away from forming again when Thelma spoke. "I know that Teddy was kind of like a second family to all of us and the older kids never got to know him well. I also know he has had his problems and his Father can't stand him, but I can't just drop the subject here. Someone has to help me find him, and I had hoped Clyde and you would be that someone."

Sharon wiped her lips with her napkin. "Have you called the police?"

"Yes, but Jack intervened and told them to forget it."

"I can see him doing that," Sharon answered. "Look I'll talk to Clyde tonight and see what he says." She reached across the table and was patting Thelma's hand. "Your right dear. Someone should do something."

The ride from Santa Fe to Tucumcari took about four hours on a good day. The hot New Mexico sun was especially brutal this day, so they had stopped and put the top up on the white convertible. It sure beat riding in that noisy old truck. There was an open case of beer on the floor on Teddy's side, and about every twenty minutes Billy would ask for another and fling the empty out the window. Usually at another car going the other way, and it was always followed with his trademark war hoop and raucous laugh.

Billy Joe had been feeling especially rowdy today when they left that old silver trailer that was going up in a cloud of smoke in the rear view mirror. Teddy was glad they had left, but he would have liked to have had that picture he had lusted for so many times, tacked up above the old tattered couch. Better yet he would have liked to have had that glossy one, but he had never seen that again. He might have seen the girl in person, he still wasn't sure, and now he never would be.

The longer they drove the drunker Billy got, and the goofier he got. He was using the entire road most of the time and Teddy was hoping they didn't meet a cop. They had gone off on the shoulder several times, always followed by a spray of gravel as Billy whipped the car back on the rode. Teddy was all for fun but he was starting to fear for his own safety with Billy's maniacal driving. Just when he finally found the courage to speak up, Billy suddenly pulled over and told Teddy to drive. Teddy had no idea where he was going, but he shrugged his shoulders and ran around the car and got behind the wheel. Billy crawled in the back seat and went to sleep. He had had a busy night last night.

Teddy drove quietly, about five miles per hour under the speed limit. He had no license to drive and wanted no trouble. Besides what was the hurry? It wasn't like they had anybody or anything waiting for them in Tucumcari. At least, not that he knew about. It gave him time to think about the last two months and his plans for the future.

Teddy was at the breaking point as far as calling his Mother. In fact he was going to do just that, as soon as they got settled. He had made up his mind to talk to Billy about it. The only time he had talked about it before, Billy had stuck his forefinger in Teddy's chest and yelled "NO! Bad idea."

They were still a few miles form Tucumcari when Teddy pulled over to read a map and Billy woke up. "What's the matter kid"?

"I just wanted to make sure we were going the right way"

Billy climbed back over the seat opened the door and took a leak in the road, standing so the oncoming traffic could get a good look at what he was doing. Two young girls in a red jeep obviously delighted with what they saw, honked and waved and Billy waved his pride and joy at them in response.

Teddy could only laugh at his goofy friend.

Sheriff Clem Nash called Deputy Barney Carlson on the radio and asked him to come into the office. Barney stood in front of Clem's desk, looking bored, his hat held with both hands in front of his enormous belly.

"Barney I just got a call from Clyde Morton over in Morton Valley and he was wondering what came of your search for his brother about two months ago. Says he talked with their Mother and she mentioned calling you to look into his disappearance. Got any recollection of that Barney?"

Barney bit his lip and seemed to be thinking hard through his half closed eyes. "Yep. Yes I do. I went over to the house to meet with her and while we was talking about her son Teddy-- I believe his name was Teddy, her old man shows up and tells me to get the hell out of there."

"Her old man, would that be Jack Morton?"

"Yes it is. The guys an asshole, but on the other hand the kid was a loser also. I looked up his rap sheet and it's a mile long and the shithead is only fifteen."

"Yes, well shithead or not the kid is a juvenile who's been gone for over two months. You better get back on that Barney and I want a report on my desk by tomorrow night."

Barney said nothing. He just turned and walked out. He had a super case of heartburn to go with the burning sensation Clem had just put in his ass. He popped a few Tums in his mouth as he stood on the courthouse steps. Then shaking his head in disbelief he walked around his cruiser and more or less fell into the drivers seat. Time to go back to Morton Valley, like it or not.

Tucumcari was a small town in comparison to Santa Fe. It seemed to be broken up into many little neighborhoods nestled in red rock hills. The architecture was still mostly Spanish in style with lots of stucco and red tiled roofs in the areas where there were homes. But it had its share of seedy places too with trailer parks and one room shacks.

"We need to find a place to rent for a while kid." Billy Joe was scanning the homes for signs as the meandered in out of poorer neighborhoods.

"Why don't we look for someplace nicer Billy? We lived about as primitive as we could back there in Santa Fe and I would like a shower and a telephone and maybe some electricity."

Billy seemed to get mad at Teddy's comment. "Well look who's getting all fancy pants on me. Primitive, where did you learn that fancy word? I didn't hear no damn complaints when I took your sorry ass in. I'll find us a place and you can come with me, or go back out on the highway and stick your fat thumb out and see where that takes you."

Teddy said nothing. He only wanted to say that he was tired of living in squalor, but the last thing he wanted right now was to piss Billy off. There was a change coming over Teddy and it was subtle right now, but it was growing. He had done a lot of growing up in the last two months since he left Morton Valley. There had been a time when nobody had much hope that old Teddy had any kind of moral compass. Maybe being knocked on the head back in Denver and then shooting a person had started his resurrection or maybe it was his failed sex attempt and embarrassment that night in the trailer. Then again maybe it was just seeing how Billy Joe acted and behaved that had woken him up to what could lie ahead for both of them. He had known a good life back in Morton Valley and right now he missed his Mother so much. He wished he was home in his own bed.

"It's late kid. Let's just get a motel for tonight and well look some more tomorrow." Billy swung the car into a gravel lot with several little cabins and a sign that said, **Bernie's Modern Cabins. Cabins available by the hour, day, or week**. He went into the office and came out a few minutes later with a key.

It was dark in the cabin and Teddy could only make out a bed, a dresser and one tattered upholstered chair. He threw his bag on the floor and sat down in the chair facing the door, and waited for Billy to bring the rest of his stuff in. He was hurt and confused right now. Being confused was nothing new to Teddy but getting his feelings hurt? That was a change.

"You're pissed at me now ain't you kid." Billy had thrown his army duffle bag on the floor next to Teddy's gym bag and was now standing in front of the chair looking down at him.

Teddy just looked up at him like some kid whose dog just got run over.

"Look kid. We don't have a lot of money right now, but if things work out for us here, then maybe we could skedaddle back to Vegas and get us a nice room in one of those big hotels. I hear they got stage shows out there with lots of bare tities and girls that will do anything for a price. They got food buffets with roasted pigs and all kinds of desserts and shit. Don't that sound like fun kid? You know something else kid? I been thinking and I know you want to call your mom and all, but how about you write her a letter and tell her your all right? Then she could quit worrying about you."

Teddy smiled. This was the Billy Joe he didn't want to leave.

After they were settled in they spent the rest of the day driving around and checking out a few potential places to rob. Billy finally spoke up saying, "they had to set their sights higher if they wanted to make a good haul. No more ma and pa grocery stores. They wanted to make a killing here as fast as they could, and then move on before the cops had time to build a case on them."

Billy took the horns off the car so it wouldn't be so obvious if they were spotted driving away. That night they bought a pizza and took it back to the cabin along with a new case of beer. Then they both got drunk and passed out on the bed, which took care of Teddy's most recent fear. Sharing a bed with Billy.

Barney Carlson did not find out much when he looked into Teddy's disappearance. For one thing a lot of time had elapsed and the trail had run cold, if there had ever been a trail to start with. He did luck out on one thing. By chance he found the farmer who had given Teddy the ride to Iowa City in the back of his pickup truck.

"Kid was a little scary looking so I made him stay in the back. He didn't seem to mind much, but then I never really got a chance to talk with him, being in the back and all." Judd Kelly was standing in the Sheriffs office where he had come in voluntarily after seeing the article Barney had ran in the paper with Teddy's picture.

"Where did you leave him off?" Barney asked sticking his forefinger under his collar to ease the pressure on his fat neck.

"I dropped him off at the railroad yards south of town there. He didn't ask to get off there, that's just where I was going. Business you know."

Barney waved his fat hand at Judd, as if that was more information than he needed.

"Never saw him again after that" Judd continued, "But hell I wasn't looking for him either if you know what I mean. Did he do something bad cause he sure looked like the kind that could raise hell? Had a mean damn look on his face, he did."

"No he's just missing and we are trying to find him. Thanks for coming in Judd and if you think of anything else, get a hold of me will you?"

Barney sat down in his chair thinking to himself. *Well that was that, and that was also about as far as I am going to go with this. I ain't no goddamn detective and never wanted to be. Sheriff can find someone else to do his nosing around. That kid isn't worth all of this time and trouble.*

Teddy saw the gun on the table when he woke up. Billy Joe was in the shower singing some Elvis song. *He sounded like Elvis would have sounded if someone was trying to ram a beer bottle up his butt while he was singing.* The random thought made Teddy laugh.

Teddy was no longer nervous about robbing people. They hadn't had anything happen, that they could call close to getting caught. It seemed like people just didn't give a shit about getting robbed. The gun made them nervous though, but Billy had never really threatened anybody with it. Just stuck right there in the front of his pants were they seemed to get the message, but the law of averages was against them in the long run and Teddy knew it. As soon as he had enough money he was going to call it quits.

A problem had surfaced that was not helping his financial situation. Last night Billy had made him chip in on the room expenses and that was the first time he had to pay for anything.

"Were going to be looking for bigger and better jobs," Billy had explained. "This penny ante shit we been doing is not cutting it kid and there is no way we are going to get to Vegas unless we hit a few big ones. Today's job," he was explaining was a Dairy Queen that he had stopped at yesterday afternoon. "It ain't going to be the mother lode but that cash drawer was full when I was there and there was only two little pimple faced broads working there. Should be a piece of cake. Lets get to work."

Teddy parked behind the building again with a clear shot out of there and down an alley.

"This will be quick kid" Billy quipped as he stuffed the pistol in his pants, lit up a smoke, and getting out sauntered around the building. Teddy knew his procedure. If there were people in the building, Billy would stay outside and look like he was finishing his cigarette. The lot had only one car in it parked in the back. The front lot had been empty. At three thirty in the afternoon, this would not be their busiest time.

A set of bells over the door jingled as Billy walked in and the same two girls that had been there yesterday came out from the back room giggling at something.

"Can I help you? Oh my God!--." The young blond girl of about fifteen said. Her mouth was hanging open as Billy flashed the gun and pushed a cloth bag across the counter.

"Put the money from the cash drawer in here," he said indicating the bag. He had the gun in his hand but not pointing it at them. The girl who had spoken to him broke down crying and the other one shorter and chunkier with long black hair followed suit, only much more obviously distressed then her partner. She collapsed on the floor her legs folding under her looking up at Billy and screaming. "Please don't hurt us. Please don't rape us or hurt us."

"This ain't no damn rape this is a stickup. Now you," pointing at the blond, "put that money in that bag like I told you, or I will hurt somebody."

This only made the one on the floor more upset, and now she held her head in her hands and wailed. "Oh my god I just knew this would happen some day Darla."

Billy ignored her and talked to the girl who was stuffing the bills in the bag. "Darla that your name?" She was sobbing softly but she nodded her head yes.

"That's a pretty name and you're a pretty girl. Is that all of it?"

She shook her head yes and closed the drawer, her blond pony tail bobbed up and down as she moved. She handed Billy the bag.

"Good, thank you, and now make me a banana split and I don't want any of that pineapple shit in the center. Let's see," he looked up at the menu board. "Make it butter scotch."

"You shut the hell up." Billy screamed at the girl on the floor. He was getting irritated with all of her carrying on. "Ain't anybody going to touch you. You're carrying on like I was planning on ripping your clothes off. Well I won't touch you if you asked me too. Hell, I bet you ain't even got hair on your little monkey yet. Now stand up and shut up or I will come back there and pull your pants down and give you a damn good spanking instead."

The girl stood up and tried to compose herself, her hands were hiding most of her face like she was playing peek a boo with Billy.

The first banana split the blond girl made she dropped on the floor as she was shaking so badly, but she got herself together and made another one, getting it right the second time. Billy reached over the counter and took it from her shaking hands. Both girls stood behind the counter now, the hysterical girl hiding behind the other one looking over her shoulder.

"How much was this?" Billy asked, holding the ice cream up high. They didn't answer him but Billy was looking back at the menu board.

"Ninety nine cents," Billy said shaking his head. "I remember when they was fifty cents and twice as big." He was digging in the moneybag and came out with a couple of one-dollar bills. "There's for the banana split and here's a tip for you beautiful. Darla. He shook his head and clucked his tongue. "Your going to be a heart breaker, yes you are." He winked at the little blond and she smiled shyly.

"You girls count to five hundred and then you can do what you want, but if you call the cops and they don't catch me, I will be back, and then I just might do something bad. Understand?" He grabbed his crotch and thrust his pelvis at the dark haired girl. She held her hands to her mouth and moaned. Billy Joe turned and ran out the door.

Teddy saw Billy coming around the building and moved the car towards him to meet him, but instead of jumping in the passenger's side Billy came to the driver's door.

"Slide over kid I got you something." He thrust the banana split at a surprised Teddy and they drove off down the alley like they were going for a Sunday drive.

"I almost felt sorry for those kids," Billy said. "I know it wasn't their money I took, but they were scared out of their panties, and speaking of that kid, do I look like a pervert or something? Them girls thought I was going to spread them out right there on the damn floor and rape them both. Go figure that. I might be bad, but not that bad, huh kid?"

Teddy could only laugh. The ice cream tasted so good.

CHAPTER NINE

Jack had been awfully quiet for about a week now. He really didn't want any harm to come to Teddy but on the other hand, he was fond of his newfound freedom without Teddy around. There were no more surprises, no more arguing and fighting on those long drives to school. He had told Thelma that he was sorry for not being more supportive of her and they had come to a somewhat silent, uneasy truce.

The word about Teddy was out all over town right now, and people would stop at his office in the bank offering their sympathies and Jack played the part of the grieving father to the tee, even though he didn't feel the part the way he should. That's why he was playing it low key right now. Now was not the time to say the wrong thing, so what was left unsaid was best said.

He hired a private detective to look into Teddy's disappearance. It was his way of doing something for Thelma without involving any of his time. Tonight they both undressed silently, each on their own side of the bed, while getting ready for bed.

"Barney Carlson was here today Jack. You do remember him, the Sheriffs Deputy that came that night and you told him to leave?" There was a question mark on her face as she looked over her shoulder at Jack, but her voice had been subtle.

Jack was quiet for a second and then replied calmly with just a hint of exasperation. "What did he want?"

"He wanted to tell us that he is looking in to Teddy's disappearance again. That the sheriff said he had received a complaint from Clyde about why nothing was being done."

Jack stood up his shoulders were slumped. He walked around the bed and sat down next to Thelma who was sting there in her underclothes.

"Look Thelma not a day goes by that I don't think about Teddy. I admit that you and I don't share the same views of him. You are so much more forgiving of all of the things that boy has done to bring shame on this family, but you're right, he is my son. Our son, I mean and I promise you that I will do whatever I can to bring him home."

They both laid back on the bed and turned on their sides facing each other. Thelma kissed him softly and Jack kissed her back and stroked her hair. Then they finished undressing each other and did what they had not done for a long, long time. After they had finished Thelma laid there in Jacks arms for a while thinking about and questioning Jacks sincerity. "Jack do you care if I go to Iowa City once more and look for him?" There was no answer. Jack was asleep. Thelma had never got the chance to tell him what Barney had said-- and the thing that bothered her most about that. He'd never asked.

They had done well on the Dairy Queen holdup, or at least that was what Billy had told him. He did give Teddy sixty dollars, which was more than he usually received. It had lifted his spirits a little but after a few days he was a having the doldrums again and Billy could sense it.

They had gone out for supper and were driving back on Saturday afternoon when Billy started telling Teddy about a pawnshop he had scoped out.

"Damn place sits right out in the open, in a little shopping center, so it's hard to be very sneaky, but the good thing is its open on Sunday and the rest of the stores aren't. I figure we will get there first thing in the morning. That's when they have the most money on hand and the least people around. Lot's of Mexicans go there and they're all Catholic's so they go to church on Sundays. This time you need to come in with me, because there is more than one employee and I can't watch all of them."

"So what you want me to do, just stand there? I don't have no gun or nothing."

"You don't need a gun stupid. If there is any shooting to be done I will do it. I told you, you just need to keep an eye on the other employees." Billy pulled up beside the cabin and they both got out and went inside.

Teddy sat on the bed and stared at the wall while Billy went in the bathroom. *Where was this all going to end? He had got himself into something that was turning out to be a place; he didn't want to be at anymore.*

Billy came out wiping his hands on his pants and sat down next to Teddy. "You know kid I guess in all the days we've been together, I really don't know you very well. You said you come from Iowa? Big family?"

"Just four kids and my parents." Teddy wondered where he was going with this.

"You mentioned your Dad was kind of an asshole but your Mom was ok. Why is that?" Billy had lit them both a cigarette in a friendly gesture.

"I don't know why. Maybe cause my Mom isn't always hollering at me. My Dad treats her like shit also. The only one he loves is his dear son Jack who kisses his ass every day down at the bank. My Brother Clyde is ok and my Sister she just up and left so I don't really know much about her."

Billy was blowing smoke rings in deep thought. "Your old man works at a bank?"

"Not works, he owns it."

Just then there was a knock at the door. Billy got up and answered it.

It was the owner of the motel. An elderly man of about sixty, He was short and bald with gray trousers held up by red suspenders over a dirty white tee shirt. "Hey guys your rent was paid through today. Are you going to be staying longer because if you are, I need some more money."

"Sure were staying and sorry about that. Pay the man kid for a few more days he said turning to Teddy. It's your turn."

Teddy fished out a twenty and put it in the mans hand.

"Three days is twenty four son." He was looking over Teddy's shoulder at Billy when he said it. Teddy gave him another five and he said, "thanks" and left. Teddy laid awake long after Billy Joe went to sleep that night. Tomorrow was going to be his last holdup and he was going to tell Billy, right after he got his cut. If Billy kicked him out that was ok. He would have enough money for a bus trip home.

The next morning Teddy was more nervous than he had ever been before any of their other jobs. Maybe it was the fact the he had to play an active part in this one, but what ever the reason, he was really upset and upchucking from the moment he awoke. He came out of the bathroom pale and shaking to find a grinning Billy sitting in the chair. "You got the jitters kid. You sure make a lot of noise when you puke, you know that?" Billy laughed that crazy way, only he and a mule could.

"Relax Kid; everything is going to be fine. Come on over here and sit down." Billy patted the end of the bed. Then he lit them both a cigarette.

Teddy didn't really want one, but anything to get the taste of puke out of his mouth.

"I been thinking kid, maybe if things go right today, we can head over to Oklahoma City for a while That's my old stomping grounds and I know some women over there. Maybe we could relax a little and get our wicks dipped, if you know what I mean. Go see my Mama and have her cook us up some biscuits and gravy Oklahoma style. Would you like that kid?" He rustled his hand through Teddy's hair

Teddy smiled weakly and nodded his head yes.

"I also been thinking kid that maybe you should have a gun along with you this morning also, so I dug out your rifle. It's right there on the bed. You already plugged one dude with that right kid?" He reached behind him handed the rifle to Teddy. "Careful kid she's cocked and locked. That's ready to fire if you ain't figured that out."

Teddy took the rifle from him like it was radioactive, holding it out at arms length with his right hand and eyeing it carefully.

Billy checked his wrist watch. "We should get going soon kid. Here, this will settle you down." He took a pull first and then handed Teddy a pint of Four Rose's whiskey. It burnt on the way down but Billy was right. It did have a calming effect

Billy Joe drove on the way over and Teddy sat with the rifle down between him and the door. When they got back, he was writing that letter to his Mother. He would just say he was ok, and he would be home soon.

Billy was right about all of the Mexicans being in church. The storefront looked deserted. They parked right in front and then Billy went over the details with Teddy.

"The barred window way in the back is where they keep all of the money. What we want to do is get the drop on both employees, if there are two of them. Then we get them both together in that area."

"What area?" Teddy asked.

"That barred window area I just told you about. Holy shit kid. Listen up when I talk to you."

Billy went on. "I want you to stay by the front door and watch for anybody pulling up, once we're in there. If you see someone lock the door and pull the shade down before they get in. You got that?"

Teddy nodded his head yes.

"I'll go first, you count to five and then come in ok?"

Billy slipped out of the car and approached the door. Unlike other times when he left the pistol in the front of his pants he had it out in his hand.

When Teddy came in there was not two employees but three and Billy had all of three of them standing with their hands over their heads in front of the cage.

"You he screamed," at the oldest of the three men, get behind the counter and fill this bag with the cash. You and you, he yelled at the other two, sit down on the floor." The oldest man had not yet moved even though Billy had ordered him too. Teddy who never stopped moving after he got in the door was now standing with all of them. He was pointing the rifle at the ceiling, holding it loosely in his right hand, his finger on the trigger and a look of confusion on his face.

"Watch them kid, as long as you're right here now where you don't belong. I told you to stay by the door." Billy waved the pistol at the two men on the floor and then stuck it in the older mans throat. "Get back there now, before I blow your bald head off, and do what I told you."

Billy's eyes kept flashing from the man stuffing money in the bag to the front door where Teddy was supposed to be. Finally he grabbed the bag and told Teddy to get in the car. He was only too happy to leave.

Teddy was already in the car when Billy came rushing out. He jumped in the driver's seat while throwing the money on the floor on Teddy's side. Billy looked agitated and his face was flushed but he wasn't saying anything. He was still going quite fast backwards when he threw the car in forward gear and with tires burning and screaming they were off and up the street.

The convertible top had a plastic back window, so there was no sound when the bullet came through the back window, but the windshield was another story as it exploded in their faces. Teddy turned his head to avoid the splattering glass and he could see the man Billy had just threatened, standing on the sidewalk, aiming a rifle at them, just as a second shot must have hit the trunk lid because there was an awful bang in the back of the car and Billy whipped the car around the next corner screaming like a mad cowboy breaking a wild mustang.

"Man kid. That was close. Let's get the hell out of here."

As soon as he turned the corner he turned again and again. Then he slowed down and they were in a residential neighborhood.

"Where we going?" Teddy asked. "Shouldn't we be getting out of this area?" Teddy felt of the bag of money between his legs and it felt pretty full.

"We got to get rid of this car kid. They're going to be looking for it."

"What we going to do, walk?" Teddy asked.

"No dumb ass. Where going to steal another car just like I stole this one, but yes, we might have to walk a way to find one."

Billy pulled into an alley entrance. He had to get the car off the street. He cruised slowly through the alley looking for another car. Then he saw an elderly man washing a white Ford Crown Victoria by a stucco garage. Billy pulled up and stopped while the old man eyed him suspiciously. "Here's our new wheels kid," He muttered.

They left the Mercury sitting where the Ford was and drove off, the old man who had been washing the car was in the back seat crying and pleading with Billy not to kill him. He had thick glasses that only magnified the tears coming out of his eyes. Teddy felt sorry for him and told him they weren't going to hurt him, but Billy just glared at Teddy as if he had spoken out of turn so Teddy shut up. They drove up a winding road into some foot hills that ended at a huge radio tower and parked next to it.

"Get out," Billy ordered the old man waving the pistol in his face. The man was now openly crying and pleading for mercy. Snot and tears were running down his face and his hands were shaking violently. He stumbled and fell but Billy lifted him up by his collar and pushed him over under the tower. He made the old man take his boot laces out and tied his hand behind him around one of the steel supports. Then he put the pistol to the mans temple, and pulled the hammer back. There was a soft sigh that seemed out of place and the man slumped over. There was no shot, he had either fainted or had a heart attack. Billy jumped back in the car, spun them around and drove down the road they had just come in on.

CHAPTER TEN

The Robbery and all that had gone wrong, only served to convince Teddy it was time to leave Billy and go back to Iowa. They had done quite well. The take being slightly more then two thousand dollars, of which Teddy got four hundred, but there was no amount of money that could make him do that ever again.

Billy was convinced however that they were a hot item in these parts so the next morning before Teddy could get up the courage to talk to him about quitting and going home; they were on their way to Oklahoma.

Teddy rode in silence most of the day as they meandered across Texas avoiding the main roads. He knew what he wanted to say but he wasn't going to say it while Billy was driving. That night they stopped in a little town just outside of Amarillo Texas. Billy spent the money for a night at a Howard Johnson Hotel. It was Teddy's first taste of modern living in a long time.

They swam in the pool and ate steaks at a posh restaurant before retiring to their room for the night. They had one other amenity that pleased Teddy a lot. Separate beds. Long after Billy had fallen asleep in a drunken stupor, Teddy stared at the ceiling and tried to muster the courage to make a decision on when and how he was going to tell Billy of his plans. He got back up and went in to the bathroom and wrote his Mother the letter he had been putting off way to long.

Dear Mom. His handwriting was not real legible but it was the best he knew how. **I want to tell you that I am all right. I wisht now that I was home again, but right now the man I am with is scaring me and I will have to be careful, what I say or do. I done something's that was stupid and bad. I want to quit that and be better. I will write you some more, but when I don't know. Love Teddy.**

He put the note in an envelope he had found in the nightstand sealed it and shut off the light. Outside of their room he could still hear people in the pool splashing around and playing. Billy was snoring on his back, his hand in his underwear as if his last conscious act had been to shelter his genitals from any harm while he slept. Teddy slipped on his pants and shoes and let himself out the door.

The clerk at the desk was reading a newspaper when Teddy approached him but he heard him and looked up, setting the newspaper down on the counter top. He was an elderly man with a whole head of white hair and his face looked like a road map full of wrinkles, but his smile was warm and friendly.

"Can I help you?" He asked Teddy

"I just want to mail this letter" Teddy said, "and I don't got a stamp."

He took the envelope from Teddy. "I can sell you a stamp son but you need to address this envelope to someone." Teddy looked a little perplexed for a moment.

"Will you write it on for me? I don't write that good."

"Sure where is it going and to whom?"

"My Mom in Morton Iowa. Her names Thelma Morton."

"Do you have an address?"

"Sure it's Prairie Street."

"Any numbers?" he was chuckling at Teddy and that was embarrassing him.

Teddy was looking confused again. "Most address have numbers son."

"Just Morton Iowa, I guess is all."

He wrote in big bold letters, **Thelma Morton, Morton Iowa** and said "hold on I have to get a stamp." He was gone for a few minutes and Teddy's eyes fell to the newspaper on the counter. There were some small headlines that read. **New Mexico authorities looking for armed robbers. Pair are also suspects in the death of an elderly Tucumcari man.**

"That will be three cents son."

Teddy fished in his pocket and found a nickel. "Thank you Teddy stammered," he wanted to read more of the newspaper article but the man had picked the paper back up and sat back down in his chair. Teddy started walking back to his room.

"Son," the man said.

Teddy turned back around.

"Do you want your change and do you want me to mail it for you?"

"Can you," he said.

"Sure and here," he gave Teddy two pennies.

Their room was around the corner from the Inn Keepers desk and when Teddy was almost there he saw that the lights were on. *Shit Billy must have gotten up.*

Teddy stopped for a second to think. *What was he going to tell Billy? He would say he was thirsty and went to get a pop. Yea, that would make sense.*

When he came in the room Billy was in the bathroom peeing, but the door was open. Teddy went right for his bed and crawled in clothes and all. Billy came out of the bathroom rubbing his eyes and sat down on the end of the bed and lit a cigarette. He inhaled deeply and then said. "Hey kid, wake up, we got to talk."

Oh shit. He is going to kill me if he finds out about that letter. Teddy was feigning sleep, not knowing if Billy knew he had been gone or had something else on his mind.

Billy walked over to Teddy bed and shook him. Teddy sat up looking surprised but keeping the bed covers up so Billy would not see his pants. "What?" He looked surprised.

Billy sat down on the edge of the bed.

Oh shit here it comes. He had already forgotten the story he had made up. *A bottle of pop. Yes he had gone for a bottle of pop.*

"You know, I been thinking kid." He took another big drag on his cigarette. "We did all right on that job back in Tucumcari. We need one more big one and then we can go to Vegas like I talked about."

He didn't know I was gone. Now if I can explain why I got my pants and shoes on I might be all right. Teddy pulled the covers up higher and slid his feet away from where Billy was sitting.

"Something big kid, like a savings and loan, or a bank or something."

Teddy who had been propped up on one arm moaned and slid back down in the bed.

"Billy laughed and patted his leg. "You're tired kid. We'll talk more about it in the morning. I got to go buy some more smokes. He stood up buttoned his pants and tucked his shirt in. Then looking in the mirror he smoothed his hair back, reached over and shut off the lights and slipped out of the room.

Teddy ran for the bathroom and threw up the best steak supper he had had in ages.

Thelma had gone back to church to pray for her lost son. It was about all she could do right now with Barney's investigation seemingly out of steam and out of evidence. Barney had stopped by and told her and Jack about the man in the pickup truck taking Teddy to Iowa City and dropping him off at the railroad crossing. He shook his head sadly and said "the trail had gone cold from there."

She had become convinced that no one in Morton ever wanted to see Teddy come home. That included Jack who was giving her some kind of lip service and Clyde who had seemed to want to help her at first, who now had gone quiet on the subject. Thelma hadn't gone back to Iowa City, even though she'd talked about it, and Jack had said he would drive her. She remembered how futile her search had been before in Iowa City and what evidence did she have to make it seem, going back there would be any different this time.

So on this hot July Sunday morning she sat about halfway back in the church and listened to the Reverend T.B. Whistler, as he talked about the parable of the prodigal son. *He must have known I was coming and picked it out just for me. It was too fitting to be a coincidence. Just another kick in the ass.* She thought.

T.B whistler seemed to be looking her way, way too much in his fiery oration. Pounding his pulpit and waving his well-worn bible at his captured audience. Thelma was only too happy that he had a long black gown on over his clothing, because she was almost sure that his pants were unzipped and his eyes were not the only things looking her way. She slid over in the pew a foot or so, hoping to hide behind a tall man in front of her.

Jack on the other hand had something besides Teddy on his mind this morning. He told Thelma that he was working on a merger with a bigger bank in Des Moines and would be working until early afternoon. In reality he was working on a merger with his, and Dorothy Perkins genitals. Dorothy was a very rich client of his, whose husband had left her for prettier, younger, and greener pastures. She wasn't the most beautiful woman in Iowa but she had a body to die for and had held it too close to Jack in some of those friendly hugs of hers enough times for Jack to notice that the door of opportunity was wide open.

Jack had always been faithful to his wife in the past, but now with Thelma being consumed by Teddy's running away and ignoring him, and his own biological clock running down, those day dreams about Dorothy sitting on his desk with her skirts hiked up and her legs locked around him, were becoming more than day dreams. He wanted in her pants, and soon. Today they were having coffee and doughnuts at Dorothy's palatial estate north of town. Jack was laying the groundwork for bedding her. His efforts were clumsy at first, after all he was new to this game, but Dorothy knew all too well what his intentions were, and did her best to keep the fires in Jack's loins cooking. A woman loved to know she was wanted.

She had invited him out this morning to go over some stocks and bonds that Jack had urged her to invest in months ago. Right now she sat on the same side of the table with Jack, her ample breast pushed into his arm and an aura of expensive perfume emanating from her cleavage like a flowerily sickly mist from an ancient genies bottle. Jack tried to explain how things were going for her financially, but his train of thought was being clouded over by his own lack of blood to his brain, and Dorothy's provocative behavior. Her hand was now on his leg and creeping higher by the moment and Jacks little friend was coming down to meet her. Then the doorbell rang and Dorothy's elderly Mother walked in before she could get up to answer it. She was a diminutive woman whom the years had not been kind to, but she carried herself with an air of authority and was dressed to the hilt.

"Am I interrupting something?" She asked through her black veil hanging down from her wide black Sunday hat.

"No Mother," she smiled, "this is Jack Morton the banker and he was being so kind as to go over some investments with me."

"Well I just thought I would come over and have dinner with you dear, if that's all right, but if I am interrupting something, well you two just carry on, and I will sit quietly and watch. Maybe I can learn something," she added with a smile.

Jack had a quick vision of her sitting quietly with her purse in her lap watching him and Dorothy copulating on the table top and almost laughed out loud.

"We can finish this some other time," he smiled.

"Dorothy gave him a look that he was sure said, *"thank you and yes you do have a rain check."*

Jack gathered up his papers and Dorothy walked him to the door. Out of mother's sight for moment, she threw her arms around him and said "Thank you Jack." She kissed him lightly on the corner of his mouth lingering just long enough for Jack to sense that it was no sister kiss. Jack had felt her invitation to come back and finish up what they had started and Dorothy in their short embrace, felt something poking her, and wanted him to come back soon.

Teddy had lain wide awake most of the night nursing the rest of the quart of whiskey Billy had been working on earlier in the evening, and waiting for him to come back. He had made a decision that he was going to make the split in the morning and this time he was not going to chicken out. This thing had gone on way too long. It was no fun getting shot at and then tying up an old man up and scaring him to death. They could get caught for murder, and get caught they would sooner or later. He had heard tell that down here in Texas, they could fry your ass in the electric chair for murder. The thought made him shudder and have another drink. He didn't give a shit about going to Vegas anyway. What could he do there? He couldn't gamble or drink or go to any of the nudie shows. That would just take him farther away from home and that's where he wanted to return. He also didn't want to meet Billy's friends and relatives in Oklahoma. He would just have Billy take him to the bus stop in the morning and they could say goodbye and call it quits. He would promise Billy that he would never rat on him, cross his heart and hope to die.

Teddy had some fears that Billy may have made the split himself because he had taken his bag with him when he left, and that had seemed strange at the moment. *But come to think about it he never left him alone with his bag did he? What was in that bag was just a tall dark secret. Oh well, if he didn't come back that would just make it that much easier.*

Teddy could stay awake no longer, tired and drunk he succumbed to a fitful sleep. When he awoke it was light in the room from the sunlight coming in around the curtains. His back was to Billy's bed and the door. Someone was snoring softly and it didn't sound like Billy. He had spent too many nights in the same bed with him not to recognize that. Teddy slowly turned and was looking at the sleeping face of a young Mexican girl with Billy's tattooed arm draped over her, one hand still cradling her tiny naked breast. The other breast hid in the folds of the sheet.

She was smiling softly in her sleep as if she sensed he was looking at her, her hand went up and pulled the sheet higher around both of them but she didn't wake up. She reminded Teddy of the girl in the glossy photo back in the trailer, but much younger.

Teddy didn't want to be here when they woke up, so he took his pants, shirt and shoes and retreated to the bathroom. He had a terrible hangover and his mouth was dry so he bent over and drank right from the faucet. It had a soapy taste that threatened to make him sick so he spit the rest out. He could get a pop at the café. No more puking for Teddy.

He just sat by the pool for a while until his headache subsided watching a couple of teenagers blasting each other with a beach ball. It looked like fun and that was what he should be doing right now. Being a kid, instead of robbing people and getting drunk.

Needing a drink of something and not wanting to wait any longer he walked down to the café. It was close to noon and after losing his supper last night to the toilet, a hamburger sounded good, so Teddy ordered one up with a tall glass of cola. By the time his burger came he had finished his cola so he ordered another one and drank it slowly wasting time.

When he returned to the room the girl was gone and Billy was packing some thing in his bag. Teddy closed the door softly and sat down in a chair by the door. Billy hadn't even acknowledged him coming in. He seemed to be preoccupied with what he was doing.

Teddy cleared his throat but his words still came out strained and almost unintelligible.

"Billy I want you to drop me off at the bus depot. I'm going back home."

His back stiffened but he didn't say anything or turn around to face him. Teddy eyed the door in case he had to make a run for it. He was bigger than Billy, but Billy had the muscles of a man and Teddy was still soft and he knew it. Besides Billy might just shoot him right here in the room. He could get that damn crazy sometimes if you made him mad.

When Billy did turn around he was smiling or was it a sneer? Teddy was not sure. "Come here kid and sit down." Billy was patting the end of the bed where he was now sitting.

As soon as Teddy was sitting beside him Billy lit them both a cigarette. This was always a sign to Teddy that some words of Billy's wisdom were about to come his way. Like an old Indian Chief passing the peace pipe.

"You know kid when I saw you coming across those railroad tracks that day in Santa Fe, I wasn't desperate for company. But you looked to me like someone old Billy could trust and wouldn't screw me over." Billy took an especially long drag and blew the smoke out in a ring. "We became buddies that day kid. We became partners just like two people do when they get hitched, and tell the preacher that they will be together no matter what kind of shit comes their way. Now you want to quit when we are so close to making it big?"

Teddy had not said a word but he was sticking to his guns and whatever Billy had said so far was not changing his mind.

"Here's what I am going to do kid so listen up. You come with me on this one last job and then I will kick you loose and you will never see me again."

"What's the last job Billy?"

"I told you the other day kid, but you never listen do you? Were going to rob a bank?"

"Where?" Teddy was shaking his head no as he asked the question.

"Not sure yet kid, but I will let you know when we get close."

Teddy was quiet, still shaking his head no. "We're going to get busted Billy. Banks are big places with lots of people and you and me are going to watch everybody and still rob a bank?"

"I didn't say it was a big bank kid." He was getting heated and Teddy could sense it. "You think I'm stupid or something? You think I would try something I know we can't do. Well you listen to me kid. This will work and no one is going to get busted. Now are you in or out?"

"What happens if I'm out?"

"Not sure kid but it might not be pretty. Get your bag and let's hit the road. You're in-- you got no choice." He said angrily and pointing his forefinger at Teddy.

CHAPTER ELEVEN

The letter came on Monday morning but Thelma didn't see it until lunch time because she was at the hairdressers. When she did finally see it she was puzzled because it had no return address and she didn't recognize the handwriting. Then as she unfolded the letter inside the envelope, her eyes and her mind identified with her son's rudimentary penmanship.

Her hands were shaking and the tears filled her brimming eyes and overflowed. She held the letter to her bosom and sobbed out loud. *He's alive oh thank God. He's alive but wait. He has been abducted. What else could it mean when he says the man he is with might harm him?* She read the letter once more. Then she saw for the first time the logo on the stationary. *Where was this place in Texas?*

Thelma ran for the phone. She was shaking so hard she could hardly turn the dial and messed up the number twice before she got it right.

"Morton National Bank how can I help you?" the soft voice said.

"I need to talk to my husband right now."

"Your husband is who?"

"Jack. Jack Morton. Your boss. This is his wife so get him on the phone right now."

"Please hold."

Thelma changed ears with the phone and wiped her wet face on her sweater sleeve. *They knew where he was now, it was just a matter of having the police pick him up and then she would bring him home and---*

"Mr. Morton is in a meeting right now Mrs. Morton but he says to tell you to call back in an hour or so."

She was incensed and slammed the phone down. *That was the last straw with this pompous bastard.* She dialed the sheriff's office. *Jack Morton could kiss her ass. She would find her son and bring him home and Jack could pack his bags.*

It just so happened that Deputy Barney Carlson was in the office that day eating his third fried roll and drinking his fourth cup of coffee, when the receptionist sent the call from Thelma through to his desk.

Barney listened intently chewing and swallowing his roll. He wiped his mouth with the back of his hand, cleared his throat and told Thelma that this was a positive thing. "Clem and I were going over to Morton this afternoon anyway, so why don't we stop by and we can talk about the whole thing."

This was great. Someone was finally going to work with her. Barney said Clem was coming also, and he was the top dog. The head honcho. She wasn't even going to call Jack back and give him the satisfaction.

They drove through the panhandle of Texas and into Oklahoma. Teddy had noticed a radical change in Billy Joe. He had taken his silver plated revolver out of his duffle bag and slid it under the front seat. He chained smoked, but this time he never offered one to Teddy. In fact he seemed to ignore Teddy, answering his questions with yes or no or just shrugging his shoulders. Once when Teddy asked him to stop at a bathroom he pulled off on the shoulder of the road and told him to go there and now.

"I have to shit," Teddy said. He threw him a box of Kleenex and said "shit right here. Shit, or I'll beat the shit out of you." Teddy obliged him much to the amusement of a few passing motorists and his own humiliation.

They were to Oklahoma City in the early afternoon and Teddy was expecting they would go east to Tulsa. That was where Billy Joe's relatives were supposed to be. Instead Billy headed north on the new interstate much to Teddy's surprise. He wanted to ask where they were headed, but Billy was in such a foul mood he thought maybe he should keep quiet for now. It was extremely hot outside and they rode with all of the windows down to get some air in the car, so the wind whistling through the car made normal conversation, if there had been any, almost impossible.

Around dusk they pulled into a motel just outside of a small Oklahoma farming community. The night was almost serene with a brilliant sunset in the western sky, filtering through puffy white clouds, turned pink from the waning light. You could smell the aroma of fresh alfalfa hay that had been cut out back of the motel and it made Teddy think of his brothers Clyde's farm back in Iowa. In fact so much of Oklahoma made him think about Iowa. Gone were the mountains and red limestone cliffs they had drove through all day. It was just flat prairie land as far as you could see. Teddy missed home and his family so much. Hell he was even starting to miss his father. Billy broke the silence as he shut the car down.

"Were stopping for the night kid. I'll go get us a room and you can start unpacking our bags. Once we get settled we'll go find us some vittles."

"I'm not hungry," Teddy said. He had to assume that vittles meant food. Billy's hillbilly talk left something to be desired.

"Well hungry or not you're coming with me." The look on Billy's face, told Teddy it was no time to argue.

Barney and Clem both looked at the letter several times. Clem Nash had been the County Sheriff longer then most people could remember and was almost a fixture in the town of Morton and the County. He was a huge man with a barrel chest and heavily muscular arms that stretched the seams of his white shirt. He was getting a little thick in the middle, but nothing like Deputy Barneys huge tank. Out of the top of his tee shirt that he always wore under his uniform shirt protruded a mat of black curly hair as thick as a door matt. His almost always, serious looking face was ruddy and pocked marked with old acne scars from a long forgotten adolescence. It was the face of a man that had seen way to much sorrow and turmoil over the years, but under the physical and emotional scars, it was a caring face.

"This gives us something to work on Mrs. Morton. The chance they are still here at this motel is small but those places usually keep useful information like license plate numbers and forwarding addresses. They may have a good description of the man your son is with. They may have heard where they are heading." Clem was holding the letter as he talked.

"I'll get a hold of the proper authorities down in Amarillo right away. If you son is being held against his will, this could be a federal case and we could involve the F.B.I., but we won't know that till we catch them."

Thelma pleaded her case. "But it says right there in the letter that the man might hurt him. How much proof do you need?"

"Mrs. Morton your son left on his own didn't he? That's what I read in the report or did you ask him to leave. N0! Of course not. He's not going to hurt him." What would give you that idea?" Thelma looked annoyed at Clem.

"He hasn't been what we in the business like to call a good boy, but all of that aside, you are right--- he is a minor and we need to keep that in mind. Look, lets talk to the boys in Amarillo first and see what they have to offer."

After Clem and Barney got back in Barneys squad car, Clem put his hand on top of Barneys as he was going to turn on the ignition key. "Barney you do know, don't you that I get reelected each and every term by the support of people like Jack and Thelma Morton? You also know that you work here for me, despite the fact that you are an embarrassment to me, and the whole department I may add, only because your ornery wife is my sister."

Barney looked at Clem's restraining hand on top of his and nodded slowly yes.

"Well then I want you to get some answers for them and me and fast. You understand?"

Clem didn't wait for an answer but got out and slammed the door shut. He had a lot of stuff going on right now and this was just another time he had to cover Barney's inadequacy. He didn't give a crap if they ever found Teddy Morton but you could at least make it look like you had tried.

Billy Joe had purchased a case of beer and he was about halfway through drinking it. Teddy tried to sleep but with every light in the room on and the radio blaring, it wasn't easy and right now Billy was lying on the bed, propped up on the pillows, playing a fake air guitar while some country western singer bled out the blues on the radio.

Billy took an empty beer bottle and threw it at Teddy's back. "Wake up lard ass I know you ain't sleeping. We got one more day of driving and then we'll be there and then its jackpot time."

Teddy sat up holding a pillow in front of him to shield him from anymore beer bottles. "Where's there and what's the jackpot?"

Billy sneered at him and sarcastically said, "Your old mans bank kid." He reached over and turned down the radio.

Teddy was out of the bed now on his feet and standing over Billy. "No way Billy. No damn way. You want to rob a bank, rob anyone you want to, but you are not robbing my Dads bank." His tone of his voice was somewhere between a plead and a direct order.

Teddy heard the click before he saw the gun emerge from under the pillows. He was now looking down the business end of the barrel and the hole in the end looked as big as a culvert. Beyond that Billy's sneer had been replaced with the angriest look Teddy had ever seen on him.

Billy didn't try to get up; he just talked right from his prone position on the bed, one hand holding the pistol and the other holding a half empty bottle of beer. A cigarette dangled from the corner of his mouth, the smoke drifting lazily over his head and forming a miniature cloud over the lampshade beside the bed.

"There is one thing I will not tolerate kid and that is insubordination." He shouted the word. Now he was slowly getting up but he hadn't lowered the gun. "In the Army kid if you questioned your orders they would lock your ass up in the brig. But this isn't the damn army kid, and I got a new set of rules and here they is. Do what you are told or I will shoot so many holes in your ugly kisser that your brains will run out like they was in a damn minnow bucket." Billy had gotten up and they were nose to nose right now, the gun was square in Teddy's gut. We got an understanding or not kid?"

Teddy sat down on the bed and stared crying. Billy grabbed his hair and pulled him back up.

"Answer me ass wipe, we got a deal or not, and quit that bawling before I shoot you just for being such a shit head. Deal or no deal kid!"

"I got to live in that town Billy. Everybody knows me there. What good would it do me? I could never show my face in public again."

Billy had let go of Teddy's hair and sat him back down on the bed. "Look kid, Billy said quietly and sitting down beside him, putting the gun in his pants. Look at my face kid. Do I look stupid? They ain't going to know it's you. Were gonna wear ski masks and trench coats. We won't be there ten minutes and then I will dump your ass out side of town and you can walk home to your mommy just like old times. He made a pouted face when he said it and this time tousled the kid's hair.

Teddy was numb. He was being blackmailed and there was little he could do about it. Robberies with guns were dangerous games and people could get shot or even killed. He didn't care for his father or his brother, but he didn't want them hurt or killed.

Why did I ever tell him about my Fathers bank? What a stupid, stupid, thing to do, and now there is nothing I can do, except run away or do what he tells me and then he just might find me and kill me and go rob the bank anyway. Maybe the only way I can be sure that someone is not gong to be hurt is to be there. If I go to the authorities I will be tied to the other robberies and go to jail just like him.

Teddy laid back down on the bed closed his eyes and moaned softly. He was screwed. He was screwed big time, and he knew it.

PART TWO

CHAPTER TWELVE

AUGUST 1, 1959

They had driven all day and into the waning, evening hours, to get to Morton Iowa. The fiery sun was just setting over the hills, behind the steeple of the red-bricked Catholic Church as they pulled into town. Teddy slouched down in the seat, with a baseball cap pulled down over his eyes, even though the streets were bare and deserted, he couldn't take a chance on being recognized, though he had given some thought to jumping out of the vehicle and making a bee line for home. Had he not been in so much trouble before he left Iowa, he could have tried the mercy route. Right now he had serious doubts anyone was going to feel sorry for him. He also knew Billy had the pistol right beside him and the thought of a bullet smacking into the back of his head was not very appetizing now that he had got back home.

Teddy had told Billy about an old clubhouse he had often lived in down by the river and if it wasn't occupied already, that's where they were headed. Billy had said this morning he needed a couple of days to plan things out and had suggested looking for an empty house or better yet, making an empty house. A threat Teddy quickly headed off with his offer of the old clubhouse. He didn't want anyone else hurt by Billy Joe.

"It's the next turn and then you will have to park by that old abandoned barn and we need to walk the rest of the way." Teddy was pointing out the way.

"Hope this place ain't full of rats kid, cause I hates rats. They give me the willy's."

"I never seen any but it's been awhile since I was down there. I know some bums lived in it for awhile last winter."

"Bums like you shot back in Denver." Billy gave Teddy a big sarcastic smile.

He had forgotten about that incident and now a chill ran up his spine. *When he was afraid of getting caught for murder, he had been thinking about the old man Billy tied to the tower back in Tucumcari, not the bum in Denver. Shooting the bum was something he alone was responsible for and Billy knew about it and probably would not hesitate to use it against him.*

They took their bags and some left over chicken and headed down a narrow trail to the river. The trail was littered with beer cans and candy wrappers. An old pair of girls' underpants hung in a tree, a silent symbol of someone's conquest.

The shack was just like Teddy remembered it. Made of old refrigerator crates with handle this side only stamped on the side they were facing. It smelled musty inside and the mosquitoes were buzzing around their heads as they kicked out the garbage and settled down, on the old busted down cot that had been left there.

"You can have the cot kid. Some one must have pissed on it cause I can smell it. I'll just sack out here on the floor." They had bought sleeping bags just this morning in Des Moines so at least they would be nice and clean. Billy had also bought a pair of handcuffs and he shackled Teddy to the bed frame.

For while, after Billy had left for town, Teddy sat on the floor staring at the cuffs on his wrist and thinking about the poor man Billy had tied to the radio tower back in New Mexico. *What if he left him the same way and never came back?*

He looked around him in the one room shack. *If he had to, he could smash his way out of this. He could drag this old bed right out the door with him. He wasn't stuck here by any stretch of his imagination so what was keeping him here? He just wanted it all to end and for Billy Joe to go away and for him to go back to his warm bed. He no longer wanted to get drunk or get laid. He was just a kid and now he realized it and needed his family as screwed up as they were. He had been there and done a lot of things he had only fantasized about and it was not that much fun. Just a lot of hype over nothing really. On the other hand he didn't want to go to prison with Billy when they did get caught and get caught they would. sooner or later. That was a threat he could not ignore. For now he would just sit here and play Billy's little game.*

Billy walked down the narrow sidewalks of Morton. He had left the car parked outside of the business district about four blocks away. It was a warm August morning in the sleepy town. The bells at St. Michaels rang out for early Mass and several nuns in their black and white habits scurried across the street to the old red brick church. Inside, Father Blain Bolton finished his preparations and looked out at the few old silver haired ladies that sat patiently fingering their rosary beads and praying from their prayer books. It was the same people every day he thought wearily. Coming to repent for their frivolous sinful ways and knowing all to well that the bells of time were ringing out to them, and that same time was running short.

Billy Joe crossed the street in the middle of the block coming across right in front of the church. He nodded at the Sisters who arrived simultaneously and murmured good morning to them. They smiled and returned his greeting, looking at him with some expression of curiosity at a new face in town, but also some lack of intrepidity. Being cautious, but courteous was in their nature.

Billy walked around the corner from the church and there directly behind it was Morton State Bank, just as Teddy had described it to him.

The building was made of yellow brick, built in a u shape with the entrance right in the middle, at the end of a long sidewalk that went right up the middle between the two sides of the building. It was a one-story building with lots of windows on one side and the front. Most of the windows were covered with heavy blinds to keep people who were walking on the sidewalk outside from looking into the office areas, and on the entrance end of it, some kind of leafy ivy covered most of the brick and windows. There was a courtyard on that end, leading up to the entrance with a fountain and several trees, bushes and flower boxes scattered around and then, a couple of cement benches where people could sit down and count their winnings, or losses, depending on how you looked at it. Right now Billy sat on one of them smoking and thinking.

He had noticed when he walked around the block from the church, that there were no windows in the back of the building, just a parking lot with several cars parked in it and one windowless steel door right in the middle of it with a sign that said **Employee Entrance Only**. It appeared that the only doors in the building were the main entrance in the front and that steel door in the back. It looked like from where he was sitting right now that they had to be directly in line with each other. There was no parking lot except the one in back and it looked like customers either parked parallel in the street or walked in from elsewhere.

Billy flipped his cigarette butt in the bushes, got up and walked inside the vestibule.

As you came in the main entrance, there was a generous lobby with several small desks, where you could fill out forms or take care of paper work. Right now a janitor was emptying the waste containers and he nodded at Billy. Billy smiled back and said, "How's it going?"

He didn't answer but smiled and pushed his trash container on wheels back out the entrance Billy had just come in.

On both sides of the bank lobby, in the wings, were several offices and conference rooms, most of them appearing empty. To Billy's left as he faced the back of the bank, were two large offices that said, President Jack Morton and Vice President Jack Morton Jr. That had to be Teddy's old man and brother.

The back of the lobby was the teller counter and right now there were two women back there. One of them, a middle aged brunette in a black skirt and a frilly white blouse was talking to an elderly gentleman in a blue suit. He was smiling broadly at her and rubbing her shoulder as he talked. The other teller appeared to be just out of school, late teenager and looked kind of studious, with red glasses framing an innocent looking plain face. Right now she was counting out some coin an old man had brought in, in several coffee cans and did not look happy about it.

The older lady noticed Billy approaching the counter and broke away from her conversation and walked smiling to an empty slot in the tellers counter.

"Can I be of some help to you," she asked.

Billy fished in his pocket for a bill and brought out a twenty.

"Yes I was wondering if I could get four fives for this."

"Certainly," she said, opening a drawer in front of her.

Directly back of her Billy noticed a sign that said safety deposit boxes and it showed an arrow pointing down and around the corner. It was at the top of a stairwell that went down to another level below the bank. *That is where the vault would be.* He thought. *That's where the real money would be.*

He thanked the lady for waiting on him and turned to walk out, but not before noticing that the man in the blue suit, was now in the Presidents office sitting behind a large mahogany desk talking on the phone. *So that's what Teddy's old man looked like.*

The hot air outside, in contrast to the cool air-conditioned bank, smacked him in the face as he walked outside. *Robbing this place was going to be a cake walk.* He thought.

Barney Carlson stood on Thelma Morton's front step and pushed the door bell with his fat forefinger. She was not going to be happy with what he had found out, but Clem had said keep them informed so that's what he was doing.

He had nearly given up and was turning to go back down the steps when Thelma finally opened the door clutching her white robe to her bosom.

"Deputy Carlson. Come in please, you caught me in the shower. Please have a seat in the living room here and I will be right back." Thelma indicated with a swipe of her arm at the formal living room right off the foyer they were standing in.

Barney had caught a glimpse of a very nice breast looking up the wide flowing sleeve of Thelma's housecoat, when she made the motion. It was a small taunt breast for a lady her age. He had a small stirring in his groin as he crossed over the threshold into the richly decorated room. He had not seen his own wife's breasts in five years. They slept in separate rooms because of his snoring and she told him when he lost a hundred pounds or so, maybe she would let him get back in the saddle, but not until. Barney looked at the Queen Ann chair with its spindly legs that Thelma had pointed at. He wasn't going to take the chance, he would stand for now.

There was a white-bricked fireplace at the far end of the room with a lot of gold handled fireplace accessories sitting in front of it in a decorated stand. The hearth was marble and the mantle looked to be also, sitting on the spindly necks of two ornate swans that were built into the brick. Above the mantle was a portrait of some stately gentleman, from a bye-gone era, sitting on a white horse in a leather coat and a ten-gallon hat. Barney walked closer for a better look. The picture appeared to be from the eighteen hundreds.

He heard a rustle of clothing and hurrying soft footsteps behind him and turned just as Thelma came back into the room wearing a tan colored shirt waist dress. She was fastening the last of her hair into a bun on the back of her head as she approached Barney.

"I'm sorry for making you wait, I normally don't shower so late in the day, but I guess I got a little lazy today in getting dressed."

Barney stared at her chest for a second not being able to forget the bare booby he had just witnessed, now that she was back to remind him of it.

"No. Ah, no problem," he said. "I just have a few things to go over with you and then I will be gone. I heard back from the Amarillo Police this morning and we didn't find out a lot. The people at the motel did recognize your son's picture, so it was him that was there all right. We have no idea who the other man was. They had checked out of the room the day before."

Thelma sat down in the chair she had offered Barney, gathering her skirts around her. She had a puzzled look on her face. Her tone of voice only served to emphasize her disappointment. "Is that all they said? No idea where they went? No license plate number?"

"No nothing like that. But they did get a description of their car because another guest had taken a picture of the motel that day with his new Polaroid camera and had given the desk clerk a copy for a souvenir. There were only four cars in the lot that morning and they could account for the other three, so they think this one might be theirs."

"You make it sound like they are in something together Deputy. My son is being held against his will." Thelma had stood back up and was looking more defiant now standing and facing Barney with her arms crossed. She looked quite irritated.

Barney shrugged his shoulders while he fingered the brim of his hat. He wanted to tell her to not shoot the messenger but thought better of it. "The desk clerk said the boy was alone when he saw him that night. They talked for some time and he asked for help in mailing the letter you received. Seems to me he could have walked away if he wanted to. But look, lets not jump to conclusions. I just wanted to pass on what I did find out and we will keep looking for that car. There is an A.P.B out right now in Oklahoma and Texas so let's see what happens." Barney wanted to leave as he could feel a terrible gas problem coming on, but he needed to ask a question and it had nothing to do with Teddy. The portrait over the mantel had peaked his curiosity. "The man in the portrait above the fireplace is that some relative of yours, or just a picture?" Thelma looked irritated at the question and Barneys sudden change in subject matter, but answered curtly without looking at the picture. "That's Jacks great, great Grandfather," she sighed. "The town is named after him. Deputy, is there any evidence that Teddy and this man are doing anything wrong or are they just traveling around together?"

"We don't know Mrs. Morton but we are looking into that and you will be the first to know. Now if there are no other questions I do have to go. *Before I drop a fart in this room that will hang in here like mustard gas in the Argonne forest,* Barney thought.

Thelma deeply troubled sat back down and waved him off. "No. I have nothing else."

Barney stepped outside and promptly closed the door, quickly relieving the impending pressure in his abdomen. It had to be that damn cheap beer he had last night talking back. He walked slowly giving his pants time to air out before he got back in the squad. Maybe his wife was right. He was just a sow.

Jack was ecstatic. Dorothy Perkins had just called this morning and she had more than investments on her mind. She had asked Jack if he could get away for a night. Tomorrow night to be exact. Their last meeting had left her in a state of excitement that was not abating and she knew that she wanted Jack to fulfill a role as more than her banker. She had arranged a night out on the town in Iowa City for them, and rented an expensive suite at the Carlisle Hotel.

As soon as he hung up from Dorothy's call he called Thelma before he lost his nerve. This whole thing was very exciting to him but also a little unnerving. He had a lot to lose if it ever got out. His family name was an icon in Morton and he could ill afford to tarnish it. Yet the thrill of a new sexual adventure was something he couldn't put out of his mind, especially at his age. He had crossed an imaginary line in the sand that he had sometimes fantasized about crossing. It wasn't that he didn't love Thelma, he did. But Jack Morton was used to getting more out of life than he was entitled too and this was the last taboo. He was convinced he could have his cake and eat it too.

Thelma was listening to Jack on the phone, while standing in the kitchen leaning on the counter top and watching two Robins out the window tugging at opposite ends of the same worm. She was still irritated about the Police report from Barney. She wanted to be able to tell Jack that she had found Teddy despite the lack of any attentive action from his father. She wanted to shame and embarrass him. Right now the only thing she was hearing was Jacks explanation of a last second meeting in Iowa City tomorrow night and he might have to stay over if it got too late.

"Jack." Thelma interrupted him. "I don't care about your business plans. Never have and never will so why are you calling me now to tell me this. You go where you want and do what you will, all the time. That's nothing new"

"I just thought I would be thoughtful and tell you in case you had other plans." Jack was trying to control his temper that was a step above simmer right now.

It was time to tell him about the letter. She had kept it under wraps long enough and this whole thing was going to backfire on her so she better spill the beans. "Jack they found Teddy."

"Where? How? That's good news Thelma. How did you find this out?"

"I received a letter from him and I turned it over to the police and they traced it to a motel in Amarillo Texas."

"Why didn't you tell me about this?" He was practically shouting in the phone and he got up and closed the door to his office ignoring the stares of an elderly couple that had been right outside his door waiting to see him. "I am his father, am I not?"

"Just what in the hell do you mean by that?" Thelma was mad now also and pacing back and forth in the kitchen switching the phone cord from one shoulder to the other, every time she turned around. "You have never been a father to that kid Jack. Is it any wonder he ran away? Sometimes I would just as soon run away from you too, you-- you, pompous ass."

Jack had calmed down a little, seemingly deflated by Thelma's outburst. "Where is he?"

"They're not sure." The tantrum had made her emotional and she was crying as she talked. "They left Amarillo before the police could talk to them."

"Who are they?" Jack sounded sarcastic.

"Teddy is with some other man and they have no idea who he is."

Jack let out a long sigh. "Look Thelma I will be home for lunch and you can fill me on things then ok."

"Ok Jack," she said softly.

He hung up the phone. *Damn just about the time when things were going so well and now this. Well it's too late now to back out on Dorothy. She said she was leaving for Iowa City right away. She had shopping to do. He had a whole day to patch things up with Thelma anyway.* Jack walked over and opened his office door back up. "Mr. and Mrs. Commers. It's always a pleasure to see you and sorry about that interruption. A little trouble on the home front. Kids you know."

CHAPTER THIRTEEN

Teddy heard Billy coming back through the woods, towards the shack, a few minutes after he had heard the thump of the car door shutting, up the hill from the shack. He was making no attempt to be quiet about it. He sure hoped it was Billy and not some kids coming down here to drink beer and jerk off. His ass was getting sore from sitting on the floor chained to the end of the bed and right now all he really wanted was to get this whole thing over with. There seemed to be no way to talk Billy out of it and he could only hope that things would go as good as Billy Joe believed they would, and no one would get hurt.

"Hey kid." Billy greeted him as he stuck his head in the door. "I brought you some breakfast." Billy bent over and removed the cuffs from Teddy's wrists and then shoved a greasy brown bag at him. Inside was an egg sandwich and some fried sausage links wrapped in a brown paper towel. The grease had already congealed into the towel giving it the appearance of an oily rag. He also handing him a carton of warm milk. He had a similar sack for himself except in place of milk, he had a beer.

"Thanks" Teddy said.

"No problem kid. You're not mad at me for tying you to that bed are you?" he didn't wait for an answer. "It was for your own good kid. Hey listen, I was in your old mans bank and that place was just made to be robbed. I think I saw your old man sitting in his office, talking on the phone like some big ass, big shot, in his fancy pants and lily-white shirt. My daddy used to call those kinds of people stuffed shirts. All full of themselves and thinking they are so God all mighty. He won't be so smug tomorrow when we relieve him of some of his money."

"Tomorrow?" Teddy's face held the question as he looked at Billy while chewing a sausage.

"Yeah, tomorrow morning kid. Ain't no use waiting any longer and I'm tired of living here in this pissy smelling old shack. How the hell you stayed here is beyond me. I ain't no fancy pants kid but this place is worse than living in a city dump. You know what kid? Tomorrow is Tuesday and that's my lucky day."

Billy laid out his plan, while Teddy sat and listened. They would get there first thing in the morning, right at 9 a.m. the less people they had to deal with, the better.

"How early does your old man get there Teddy?" Billy belched and threw his empty beer bottle against the wall. It bounced off with out breaking.

"Dad always opens up," Teddy answered. Either him or Jack. I don't think anyone else even has a key."

"Who's Jack" Billy opened another beer.

"My older brother. He's the vice president. My father thinks the sun rises and sets on his ass. I hate him."

Teddy's skepticism for Billy was being replaced with cynicism for his father and brother again, and Billy could sense it. That was a good sign, as he felt Teddy had been going soft on him.

"Well when I was there today there was no Jack there. Just two women tellers and your old man and--- oh yea, some old wino, trading in all of his pennies for some money to buy some hooch. If there are people in the bank tomorrow were going to lock them all in the vault so they can't call the cops on us. Not until we get out of there anyway. Have you ever been in the vault?"

Teddy nodded his head yes.

"What's it look like in there." Billy lit two cigarettes and handed one to Teddy. He hadn't done that for a few days.

"Just a room with lots of drawers."

"Locked drawers?"

"Yes-- but the tellers and Dad always have keys for them." Teddy inhaled deeply on the cigarette. He hadn't had one for a few days and this one tasted really good, but when this was over he was quitting.

"Does the vault have a big safe door?"

"Yeah, but it's always open during business hours. The safe deposit boxes are in there, so people need to get in there to get at their stuff."

91

"How many safe deposit boxes are there?"

Teddy thought for a second. "I don't know maybe a couple of dozen."

"What's in them? Jewelry and shit like that?"

"How the hell should I know Billy? I never looked in any of them. That's why they are called safe deposit boxes." He was getting tired of Billy's questions. He squashed his milk carton and tossed it in the corner and then followed it with his cigarette butt that landed in a shower of sparks.

Billy went over and stomped on it. "Hey kid. Don't set the shack on fire yet, we got one more night here you know."

By the time Jack got home for lunch, Thelma had had time to simmer down a little. She had made him some soup and cut up some summer sausage and cheese with a plate of crackers. They sat on the opposite sides of the table across from each other.

"Look Thelma," Jack said between slurps of soup. "Your right I haven't been a very good dad to Teddy and I'm sorry you have been left holding the bag on this. I do care about the kid it's just----."

"Just what Jack? Just to much of an interruption in your busy day down at the bank." She paused for a second and a tear ran down her face. "I'm sorry Jack. I just want him back safe and sound. I'm sorry for going off on you."

Jack reached across the table and took her hands in his. He was feeling a little self- conscious right now. Not about Teddy, but about his impending date with Dorothy Perkins's. He had never screwed around on Thelma before and it wasn't too late to back out now. The little man in his head said he should dump the whole plan and behave himself. The little man hanging between his legs said go for it. He had to figure out whom he was going to listen too.

"Do you have the letter" he said?

"No I gave it to the Deputy."

"What exactly did it say?" Jack was still holding her hands. He reached up with the back of his right hand and wiped the tears from her face. Her skin still felt so soft. Her eyes were likened to wet pools of emeralds.

Thelma smiled at his gesture. "It just said that he wanted to be home. That he was sorry for running. That he was afraid of the man he was with right now."

"Do you think he was being held against his will?"

Thelma gave him another soft smile. "I don't think so Jack. The people that saw him in Texas said he had every opportunity to leave if he wanted too. There has to be some other reason, but I don't know what that could be." Their eyes met and for a brief moment Thelma thought that just maybe, just maybe, Jack was really caring this time. It had been so long since they'd had time for each other except for the other night when he had his way with her for about ten minutes. She walked around the table and this time she reached for his hands. He turned sideways in his chair his elbow knocking over the rest of his soup but neither of them seemed to notice. She pulled him to his feet. "Jack how long has it been since you wanted me. Wanted to hold me, kiss me, and really make love to me. Not what you did the other night."

The little man in Jacks head was now standing on his bully pulpit, screaming in the back of his skull. *How in the hell can you even entertain a thought about Dorothy Perkins, when this woman who has stood by you all of these years is asking you Jack Morton to take her in the other room and show her how much you really care. To undress her and tell her how beautiful she still is. To be one with her once more just the way you were when you created Teddy. You're an asshole Jack Morton. You're a self centered, egotistical asshole.*

Jack was confused. A part of him wanted to take her in the next room and make amends, but wait, the other man was talking back. *This thing with Dorothy was not just about sex. Hell maybe it had nothing to do with sex. Sex was just a means to the ends, and the ends were Dorothy Perkins money, safe in his bank. Lot's of her money. She just drove a stiff bargain, no pun intended.*

"Thelma lets do this." Jack murmured. "I have that meeting out of town tomorrow, but lets take Wednesday off and just you and I go some place for a special night. Maybe we could go down to Des Moines. I hear they have a riverboat supper club there that is out of this world." He kissed her lightly.

"I would like that Jack. I would really like that." She kissed him back. A full mouth wet kisses that made Jack's little man stir in his nest. I'll make the reservation she smiled.

Jack drove slowly back to the bank. He had some tall thinking to do. He was somewhere that he didn't want to be and there seemed to be no way out of it.

Barney tried to talk to the authorities in Texas at least twice a day for updates, but the news was not forthcoming. It was like they'd disappeared off the face of the map. The only additional thing he did learn was about the car. It was a nineteen fifty-six Ford Crown Victoria, two-door hardtop red over white. The lab was also able to determine from the grainy picture that the license plates were from New Mexico although they could not make out any numbers. A check with New Mexico authorities did mention that a similar car was stolen in Tucumcari a few days back and the owner had been found dead, tied to a radio transmission tower. At his residence a white fifty-six Mercury convertible that had been stolen in Santa Fe had been found and was being searched and fingerprinted. They hoped to have more on that car soon.

As for right now he was in Morton, slowly cruising the streets and letting his breakfast, which had consisted of four eggs and a pound of fried ham, washed down with a pint of black coffee settle in. He drove by Thelma and Jacks house up on the hill but didn't stop. He had nothing new to tell them. Just the sight of the house brought back visions of Thelma's perky little naked breast. It was something he would ever forget.

He drove downtown and cruised by the bank. He could stop and say hi to Jack Morton, but he never liked the man so why upset himself. Finally he drove back out to the highway and headed back to the office.

Jack wrestled with his thoughts all afternoon at work. He was so preoccupied that he could hardly function. He had to go to Iowa City to save the account, either tonight or tomorrow night, but a part of him did not want him to have sex with Dorothy Perkins. Another part of him said if he got in the same bed with that woman, it was going to happen. He could lie and say to her "he wasn't able to perform," but there was a part of his anatomy that was going to have the deciding vote in this matter and an erect one did not lie, and he had no idea how he could control that from not happening. He could be more truthful and tell Dorothy that he had reconsidered and would not cheat on his wife but it seemed he had already crossed that bridge a week ago out at her house. Either way she might just pull all of her money out of his bank and look for another horny banker elsewhere. He had never studied Shakespeare, but the words, *Oh what tangled webs we weave, when first we practice to deceive,* seemed very prophetic right now.

As for Thelma she had been deeply touched by Jacks sentiment. When he had looked at her across that table at lunch, his concern had seemed so genuine. When he had reached up and wiped the tears from her face that gesture had been so endearing to her, that it brought back memories of a caring Jack that she had fell so hopelessly in love with so many years ago. A Jack that had ceased to exist and she may have well had something to do with that. True, Jack, Teddy and her hadn't been on the same page always but losing her son was one thing, losing her marriage was another. Now she sat at the kitchen table listening only to her breathing and the ticking of the clock above the stove. She felt flushed and warm. Jack had awakened something that hadn't been active for a long, long time and she was not going to wait until Wednesday night. Yes they would go to Des Moines, but tonight, well tonight was going to be very special. She had completely forgotten about Jacks out of town meeting or hadn't been listening when he told her.

She cleaned up the spilled soup and dishes and then tearing off her clothing on the way to the bedroom, Thelma turned the shower on. She was going to go shopping and get her hair done. This evening was going to be the start of something good and she wanted to look her best for Jack. While she waited for the shower to warm up she preened in front of the bathroom mirror. She still looked good even if she had to say so herself. Despite carrying four children, her stomach was flat and her hips seemed to form a wonderfull sculptured valley of ivory flesh that led down through the silky forest to her special place. That's what Jack had called it when they first married. Her special place and he had visited down there on a regular basis. Her breasts, although not big, were still firm. Her nipples still had good color to them and were just the right size. They seemed to accent her breasts so well. She was working herself up to much, she better get in the shower.

It was too hot to sleep in the shack that night so Teddy stayed awake most of the night. It wasn't just the heat. The upcoming robbery had a lot to do with it also. Billy Joe had questioned him more about the bank. It seemed like he wanted to make sure he had everything straight in his mind before they would do it. He seemed to be excited about it, treating it like a new adventure instead of the serious crime that it would be.

Outside of the shack, the frogs were so noisy down by the river that it seemed there must be millions of them. Teddy gazed out the door at the sliver of moon overhead, just as it slid behind some high cirrus clouds. It would be hot again tomorrow. He thought of his Mother, probably sitting home wondering where he was. *I hope she's not sad*, He thought. *It won't be long now and it will all be over Mom.*

Billy Joe was sleeping right in front of the door. He had drunk himself into a stupor again and was out like a light lying on top of his sleeping bag, the revolver stuck in the front of his pants. It would be so easy to step over him and just leave, but Billy's threats against him and his family rang out in his head. He almost hoped they would get caught tomorrow so he could clear the slate. Even if they pulled it off they would always be fugitives and could he trust Billy to let him go free and forget about him? He was just not sure. No, the only good thing he had to do tomorrow, was make sure no one got hurt.

From the moment he walked in the back door, the aroma of chicken and dumplings and fresh buttermilk biscuits filled the air. Jack sensed something was up. It was his favorite meal and she made it so well, but she hadn't made it for sometime. It was almost eight, which was later, then Jack usually came home, but Thelma had called him at work this afternoon and asked what time he would be home. Something she rarely did if at all. He should have known then something was going on.

There was another smell he could not identify but it smelled like roses or some kind of flowers.

"Thelma," Jack called up the stairs.

"Down in a moment Jack. Wash up for dinner dear."

The phone rang and Jack picked it up. It was Dorothy.

"I have the most wonderful suite Jack. I am sure you will like the accommodations when you get here. I just wondered when you would be arriving."

Jack was unnerved he had forgot about her. Damn. She'd called him at home. "Look I will have to get back to you on that. Let me call you tomorrow. It won't be tonight something has come up. Please don't call here again." He hung up the phone and continued washing his hands vigorously at the kitchen sink. Had Thelma been on an extension? Then he heard movement behind him and turned.

She literally swept into the kitchen in a rustle of silk and taffeta. The negligee she wore was light blue and lights from the living room lamps behind her showed just enough to tell Jack that was all she had on. It had been a long time since he had seen her like this. She stayed out of reach on the other side of the table.

"Jack please sit darling. You must be famished. Who called?"

Jack sat down feeling for the chair, as his eyes wouldn't leave her body. He had never seen her this beautiful. Not on their honeymoon, not in the thirty some years they had been married. Jack was at a loss for words. "Someone from work he finally blurted out."

She walked behind him and untied his tie and opened his shirt. Her hands massaged his shoulders and lingered on his chest. "You work to hard Jack. You need to relax more." He tilted his head back to look at her and he could feel a firm breast in the back of his head. Her heartbeat reverberated through it and into his neck and, for a second he wanted to spin around and take it tenderly in his mouth but thought better of it. It was as if he was in a play she had choreographed and only she knew the script. It was no time to be impromptu. There was that fragrance again. It was her perfume and it was intoxicating. Thelma left from behind him, going back around the table and sitting down. She passing Jack the platter of chicken. He wanted to ask why, what, but he knew whatever he said it won't sound right, so he just stayed mute and enjoyed the scenery. Had she found out about Dorothy? Was this her way of fighting back? Thelma had a coy smile on her face but ate silently.

Jack had been hungry, but now he was too excited to eat. He ate to be polite forcing the food past the lump down his throat. Thelma asked him about his day but he ignored the question.

"I never dreamed you could be so desirable," he finally said.

"I have a fresh strawberry pie," she said. It was her turn to ignore him.

"Later,"

"Would you like to go upstairs?" She asked.

Jack only nodded yes, and wiped his face on his napkin and followed her out of the room and up the curved stair case to their bedroom. Each light they passed only served to give him another glimpse of her beauty. He had not been this excited for ages.

In the bedroom the covers where already turned back and one lonely candle burning on the nightstand was the only light. The heavy drapes were drawn tightly shut and the room seemed almost eerie. Thelma stopped and turned around taking him in her arms and kissing him passionately. Her tongue found his and for a brief moment they seemed to be locked in their own embrace. Then Thelma held him at arms length and reaching down undid his belt buckle. She undid his shirt and pushed it off of him, and then sliding her hands down his sides took the rest of his clothing all the way to the floor. His swollen manhood was staring her in the face but Thelma rose past it and pushed him backwards on the bed. As if she was opening a ribbon on top of a gift box, she undid the tie on her negligee and it floated away behind her.

There love making had been nonexistent for some time, and even back then it had been just a ritual they had gone through. Jack thinking he was doing his husbandly duties and Thelma thinking she too had to make an effort and be submissive from time to time, as if she owed it to him.

Tonight that had all changed. There was no need for any kind of foreplay; the foreplay had started this noon at the kitchen table. She took his wayward little man in her hand and guided it to her. Her fingernails dug into his hips as she leaned backwards getting her anatomy as close as she could possibly get it to him, twisting and turning and releasing passions and feelings she had never felt before. Jack was just along for the ride.

After their lovemaking subsided they talked into the wee hours of the morning, about their marriage and about Teddy. They both laid open their souls to each other and made a commitment to be there for each other for the rest of their days.

When Jack awoke in the morning Thelma was sleeping with her back to him and he was spooning her. Her perfume still lingered in her hair and the bedclothes, her body felt so warm and comfortable. He knew now that he couldn't go to Iowa City and it was best to let Dorothy Perkins know that-- even though he had encouraged it, she would not get laid by him. A check of the clock said eight a.m. he would have to hurry. He would call Dorothy when he got to work.

CHAPTER FOURTEEN

Teddy awoke with a start. Billy was shaking him with his foot and yelling at him to wake up. He looked at his watch and it was only seven thirty but Billy was ready to get the show on the road. "We have lots of preparations kid, so get the hell up. First thing we have to do is get all of our shit packed up and in the car."

"I could just leave my stuff here in the woods and come back and get it later." Teddy looked at him with a question mark on his face.

"No way kid, we are taking everything with us. When I drop you off it won't be that much trouble for you to take your stuff with you then."

"Where you going to drop me off"?

"How the hell do I know? What do you want me to do, leave you on your Mommy's doorstep? Just get your crap in the car like I told you."

Teddy rolled up his sleeping bag grabbed his old gym bag and starting following Billy up through the woods to the car. Billy was on edge and it was no time to get in a pissing contest with him. In a couple of hours it would all be over.

They drove to the little town of Albert, six miles away and Billy filled the car with gas and they both had breakfast. Billy had gone in the truck stop on the edge of town and purchased it to go and they ate quietly in the car. Teddy saw a couple of kids he knew from school coming down the sidewalk so he quick looked the other way, even though it was some distance from them. They were too busy horsing around to notice him anyway.

The weather had turned unusually hot for August in Iowa. The high today was predicted to be ninety-five degrees according to the weatherman on the radio, and the long range forecast called for more of the same for the next few days. Billy reached down and shut the radio off. He needed to concentrate.

By the time they finished eating it was eight forty-five, so they headed back to Morton and Billy methodically went over the final details. They would leave the car right in front of the bank. Teddy would have the rifle and Billy would have the revolver. Teddy was supposed to follow Billy in and lock the door behind him. "It has a thumb lever lock on it and whoever was in the bank, was in until were done," Billy said. If Teddy stood in the center aisle he could cover both the front and back doors. Billy would be downstairs with Teddy's Dad in the vault. Everybody else was to stay where they were, when they came in. "It will be up to you to make sure that happens kid. No messing up or you will wish you never met me. This ain't another dairy queen."

The threat ran a chill down Teddy's spine. This was a way different Billy Joe than the man he had met a few months back.

They came into Morton from the west and drove right down Main Street, going past the bank and making a right turn alongside of it. There were two cars in the employee's lot and another one just pulling in.

"Which one of those cars is your old mans?"

"None of them," Teddy said.

This unnerved Billy and he looked for a second like he was confused. "Where do you live?" he asked.

"Keep going straight down this road about six blocks and we are at the top of the hill. Here comes my dad now."

Teddy was pointing at a white Cadillac coming towards them. Jack was bent over the wheel shaving himself.

"Ain't that just rich, he lives six blocks from work, and has to shave on the way to work? I just love these hotsy totsy people." Billy made a U turn and followed Jack back to the bank. Jack pulled into the alley and parked behind the building and Billy went around to the front and parked at the curb. He reached between the seats and pulled out the rifle. "Careful kid it's loaded and ready. Safety is on. Now get your stocking cap on."

Jack was in a good mood as he pulled into the lot. He had come just that close to making a move that could have cost him his marriage. He knew now that Thelma had unknowingly pulled his balls out of the fire and now that he still had a set, he needed to use them, and call this whole thing with Dorothy off. It would be his first order of business.

As he came in the back door he noticed that already things seemed busy. Audrey Hall, his youngest teller who had just graduated from high school this spring, was waiting on an elderly man whose hands shook so badly he could hardly keep them in front of him. Emma Erickson, the other teller, was assisting a pretty dark haired woman with two young children. Emma who was in he early fifties had worked for Jack for as long as he could remember. She wore her long gray hair tied up in a bun on the back of her head and her gold reading glasses hung from a chain around her neck. Her blouse was pinned at the bodice by a sea shell broach. Jack had never seen the lady that Emma was waiting on before, which was unusual in a town the size of Morton. *Maybe a tourist* he thought.

Jack Junior in his three-piece black suit was coming up the stairs from the lower level after no doubt having opened the vault for the day. Only he and his father had the combination but he always opened it. He went straight for his office mumbling good morning to his father as he passed him. He had an early appointment and he needed to be prepared

Jack stopped a second to adjust the thermostat as it felt warm in the building. Both tellers looked over their shoulders at him and smiled. The pretty lady with the two children gave him a cursory glance. In the bank lobby Ida Parsons was at one of the little counters filling out a deposit slip. She owned the bakery down the street and was bringing in yesterdays receipts, just as she did every morning. Her white apron and hair net had become a permanent part of her wardrobe and she had a smudge of baking flower on her right cheek.

Jack, with his morning paper under his arm, turned right at the tellers counter and was heading for his office. That is until he saw the two men with ski masks on coming in the front door.

From the time they left the car, in front of the front door of the bank, which was about twenty feet away, Teddy had never been so scared in all of his life. He was claustrophobic in the ski mask and felt as if he was going to vomit any moment. He caught a glimpse of his fathers face frozen, with a look of astonishment on it, looking straight at him. Audrey Hall screamed and put her hands to her face, seeing Billy pointing his gun at her. "Everybody stay right where you are he screamed."

Emma however looked defiant and stepped back slowly a couple of steps, but not before she hit the silent alarm button under the cash drawer. The pretty woman she had been waiting on hunched down cuddled her children to her, tears running down her face already.

Billy had knocked Ida to the floor on his way past her, sending a bag full of loose change she had been counting off the counter top, and spilling it all over the ceramic floor. Ida cowered by the tiny workstation her right arm held over her head for protection while Billy rushed by her.

Teddy did what he had been asked and watched the doors, standing in the lobby a few feet in front of Ida. Although Billy had been waving his gun from the time he had gone through the door, Teddy had kept the rifle at his side as if he was ashamed of it.

"You" Billy screamed pointing at Jack with the revolver. "Get your pompous ass over here."

Billy vaulted over the tellers counter and grabbed Jack by the lapels with his free hand. "You and me are going down to the vault old man."

Jack did not seem afraid. It was more like he could not believe this was happening. This happened in Des Moines and Minneapolis, not in Morton.

Billy turned and hollered at Teddy. "Get your rifle up, and keep these people in line. Did you lock that damn door like I told you?"

Teddy walked back and reached behind him to click the lock shut but it was already locked. That puzzled him because he didn't remember doing that. He brought the rifle up to his chest.

Billy hollered again, over his shoulder as he walked away with Teddy's father and brother. "Don't stand in front of the door where anyone can see you lard ass. Me and the big man here have a date downstairs." Then he noticed Jack Jr. who had been in his office trying to hide behind the door. "Get out here you son-of-a bitch. You're coming too."

The alarm system had been installed about a year ago. What it did was send a silent alarm to the Sheriffs dispatch center at the county. The protocol was for the dispatcher to call the bank and ask for the code. This was a five-digit number and who ever answered had to provide that number or a car was dispatched to the scene.

Kelly Carson was the dispatcher on duty and felt that this was just another test but she followed the book and dialed the banks number. The phone rang several times because no one upstairs wanted to move to answer it. It also rang in the vault where Jack was busy transferring bundled bills into bags, while Jack Jr. went ahead and opened all of the drawers.

Billy was not sure what to do at first but then thought if no one answered the phone maybe they would think there was trouble. "Answer it" he said to Jack.

"Morton National Bank this is Jack Morton."

"Yes, Mr. Morton. This is the county Police and Fire dispatcher. We have received an alarm from your bank and we were wondering if you would provide us with the proper code."

Billy had been listening with him, almost ear to ear. "Give her the code," he said.

"Ah, It's five six one three five." The cold steel of Billy's gun was pressed into the back of his neck.

"Would you repeat that one more time sir."

"Five six one three five." Jack repeated

"Thank you sir." The connection was broken.

"Why did they call?" Billy shouted.

"Just a test, Jack countered, the alarm system calls in a test every day," he lied.

Now on the radio Kelly called squad twenty-six. Barney and Clem had been on their way to Morton to serve a warrant and pick up a repossessed car. "Twenty-six" Clem answered.

Sheriff we received an alarm from the Morton bank and when I asked for the code verification they didn't provide me with the correct one.

"Ok Kelly, were just about there. We'll check it out."

"Swing by the bank when you get in town Barney. Kelly says they got an alarm and they gave her the wrong code."

"Those dumb shits do that all of the time Sheriff."

"Swing by anyway Barney; it ain't that far out of our way."

Barney shook his head sideways but said nothing. He hated it when the sheriff was riding along.

Jack and his son were working feverously with Billy screaming at them to hurry.

Jack Jr. kept saying over and over that he was, "doing the best he could. Please don't hurt me," he pleaded. "None of this money means anything to me."

Jack Senior looked at his son with disdain. To cooperate with these people was only prudent, but to turn into a groveling, whimpering coward was pathetic.

Upstairs Teddy hadn't said a word. He just stared at the four women, two crying children and the old man who now seemed to have settled into a group in front of the teller's cages even though Teddy had not given them permission to move. For one thing Audrey was helping the women with her kids and Emma seemed to be tending to Ida who had hurt herself when she fell.

Teddy stared at Audrey. He knew her from school. She was two years ahead of him but they had been in study halls together and he'd shared a locker next to her. They had not really talked much, except to say hi and goodbye, but on one occasion when kids were teasing Teddy, and after she had gone to work for his father, she had stepped in and told them to leave Teddy alone. She seemed to be a popular girl although she was far from attractive. She had a boyish figure and glasses that didn't do justice to her looks at all. He sure was glad she couldn't see who he was. The two kids had settled down as Audrey had given them free reign of the candy jar that sat on top of her teller cage. Their Mother looked concerned but thankful for Audrey's help. Ida had stopped crying and she and Emma talked softly to each other. They had known each other for many years.

The old man seemed to just stand and stare at Teddy. His hands seemed to be shaking worse and he had a twitch in his neck that caused him to tilt his head from side to side rapidly. He still held the coffee can with all of his coins, tight to his chest and you could here the coins rattling when his hand shook.

What the hell was taking so long? Teddy walked over and peeked out the draperies in the window behind him. The streets seemed to be deserted except for two women that were cutting across the street heading for the bank. One of them was carrying a bank bag under her arm. Then reached the front door and then finding it locked they were standing outside looking puzzled. Teddy could hear them talking. They were right outside of the lobby window he was now standing by.

"They always open at nine. I wonder what the problem is." The one with the bank bag shielded her eyes and peered through the door. "There are people in there just standing there. You don't suppose there is trouble in there do you?"

"Maybe we should go back and call the bank," the other women said. They both walked back where they had come from.

Teddy was getting more nervous and more confused by the moment. *What if the people up here simply walked out? If Bill didn't come soon he was thinking about just making a run for it himself. Piss on Billy and his big ideas.*

Then he saw his father's head as he reached the top of the stairs. His brother was right behind him and Billy had a large canvas bag slung over his shoulder.

"Everybody come here," he said. "Not you," he screamed at Teddy who had started walking over also.

"Alright listen up." The kids had started crying again at Billy's shouting voice.

"Shut them little bastards up," he said to the woman. She picked up one of them and Audrey took the other.

"Now you are all going downstairs and until we are gone, you will be in the vault. Safe and sound." He laughed at his little joke. "Now get moving. You can come with us now fat ass." He motioned Teddy over and they all walked down the stairs together.

"We will suffocate," the woman with the kids said.

It was Jack Senior who spoke up. "We will be fine. The vault has its own ventilation system. Just do as he says." He seemed very calm and fatherly towards the obviously distraught woman.

Teddy had stayed at the top of the stairs but he could see everything that was going on. He heard a knocking sound at the front door and peered over the teller's counters. It was Deputy Barney Carlson. Teddy's heart was in his throat. They were caught.

When Clem and Barney came into town they had driven straight to the bank, parking in the back by the employee entrance. "You know these people Barney, why don't you go around front and check things out. I'll stay here and watch this door."

"For what?" Barney asked. Clem didn't answer him just gave him a disgusted look that said. "Do as your told." He shrugged his shoulders and went around the side of the building talking to himself. Clem checked them in at the bank with dispatch on the cruisers radio and Kelly confirmed them being there.

When Barney got to the corner he started walking towards the main entrance. *Just like always there would be nothing wrong,* he thought. Suddenly Barney froze in his tracks. Parked right in front of the bank was a nineteen fifty-six Ford Crown Victoria with New Mexico plates.

"Hey Clem!" Barney was talking on his hand held radio. "You know that car that the cops in Texas were looking for. It's right in front of the bank."

"Can you see in the front door?" Clem asked.

Barney walked slowly to the door and peered in his face against the glass.

Billy and Teddy were heading for the door when Billy saw Barney before Barney saw him, and took refuge behind the same workstation that he had knocked Ida into on the way in. He threw his hooded mask off. Teddy however was right out in the open and Barney saw the rifle, big as cuff, and drew his weapon. He pushed on the door but it was locked.

The sound of the 357 going off in the bank was deafening and Teddy ducked as he saw the glass in the door spider web, but not fall out and Barney falling to the ground clutching his stomach with his left hand.

Teddy turned and saw the smoking gun in Billy's hand and that crazy grin on his face. He raised the rifle and had Billy in the sights. *This had gone far enough, and prison or no prison I am going to stop this right now.* He pulled the trigger but all he heard was a click. He racked the lever to inject another shell and then he realized. The gun was empty.

"You little bastard you were going to shoot me weren't you? Did you think for one minute that I would give you a loaded gun?" Billy was out in the open now closing towards where Teddy stood. Teddy turned to run for the back door and had taken about three steps when the bullet hit him in the back sending him crashing to the floor.

Billy, his pistol still smoking, ran for the front door but Barney had crawled behind the blue and white Ford and was now waiting for him, peering around the back wheel. A trail of blood and gore marked his path around the car. Blood was filling his mouth, coming up from his stomach. His head was spinning and he couldn't focus his eyes anymore. He fired a desperate shot back into the bank, just missing Billy and shattering the glass farther, but it still stayed in place. Billy turned and ran for the back door, kicking Teddy in the head as he ran by him.

Barney had passed out lying flat on his back.

Clem had heard the shots and pulled the cruiser up tight against the steel door and then ran around the building to help Barney, calling in on his hand held to Kelly, that they had shots fired at the bank. At the corner he saw Barney down behind the parked car on his back and not moving. He ran and dove in beside him. There was a large blood spot on Barney's abdomen and Clem could smell the putrid mix of his intestinal contents and blood oozing out of it. Barney was breathing like a horse that had just finished the derby and a pool of blood was forming under him and running toward the gutter.

Across the street the two women who had been there earlier, saw the whole thing happening and ran screaming into Finch's hardware store across the street. "Someone is shooting people in front of the bank they screamed."

Adolph Finch the store owner, and a man who looked every bit like a mountain man, told them to stay put. He grabbed a double-barreled twelve gauge from the rack behind him and slipped in two double ought buck shells. Filling his pockets with shells, he stepped out the front door, the gun raised to his shoulder.

"Stay down Adolph" Clem hollered at him. "Go, call an ambulance and keep people out of here. Watch that side of the bank for me. Clem indicated the side he had just come from, and Adolph ran over to the corner and hid behind a trash container.

Clem had given him conflicting orders and he couldn't do both. He would stay put and just hope that the gunman would show himself. He hadn't had this much fun since Korea. Someone else could call an ambulance. Right now his little town was under siege and he had a calling again. He was going to be a hero. The thought put a sadistic grin on his face.

Billy, desperate now hit the back door with all of his might, but he could not move it more than a few inches. He checked the lock again and it appeared to be unlocked. He turned it the other way but that locked it, so he put it back where it was, and it opened a few inches and then he could see the bumper of the car up against it. He was screwed.

Down stairs in the vault Jack, his son and the others had heard the gunfight upstairs but had no idea what was going on. The vault door was still open a few inches but no one was moving. Billy had ripped the phone in the vault out of the wall, before he left, but there was another one outside in a small break room, where the employees ate their lunch and they could hear it ringing. *If I could get to it I could call the police and tell them what was going on Jack thought.* He opened the door of the vault a few inches and saw Billy at the back door so he pulled it back shut.

Billy knew that the doors were out of the question but his training in the army had told him to never quit. Find another way and make the best of it. He also knew that the police out front could see him in the lobby area, so he had to stay clear of there. He had hit one of the bastards and he was now lying behind his car. Even if he did get out, getting to his car was not going to be possible. He crept over to the side of the building and into an office and pulled the blinds. He could see this huge man trying to hide behind a trash receptacle half his size, and he had a very formidable weapon, pointing at the very window he was looking out of. He stepped back.

He made his way to the other side but on that side of the building the bank joined walls with the drugstore, about half way back. If he did get out he would have to exit out the front where the cops were. A poor risk at best, but the longer he waited the more help was going to come. He would go back to the other side and take his chances with the hulk and his shotgun.

Clem was back on the radio to Kelly but she wasn't answering on his first try, so he keyed it again "Squad twenty six to dispatch for God's sake this is an emergency."

Kelly answered. "Clem what is going; on we are getting flooded with calls down here."

"Piss on those calls Kelly, listen to me and me only. Get me an ambulance, and right now, Barney has been hit bad and get me some back up."

It was silent for a while and then Kelly was back. "Ambulance is on its way Clem, but your back-up is coming from Webster. Closest car I could find."

Webster was thirty miles off. Clem moaned in frustration and changed his posture to his other side. The sun was coming over the tops of the buildings next door and the hot asphalt roadway was burning his legs. Peering inside again he saw Billy running back behind the teller counters toward the street side. "Watch close, he's over on that side," he hollered to Adolph. Two cars passed behind Clem and he winced. He had to stop traffic.

He heard glass breaking around the corner and then he heard the mighty blast from Adolph's shotgun, saw him stand up eject the shells and reload. "Take that you son of a bitch," Adolph bellowed and laughed.

My God he's enjoying this, Clem thought.

Billy was not hit but he was convinced now that, going out that side had been a bad idea and he headed downstairs.

Teddy was lying flat in front of the teller's counters. The bullet had entered in his upper back and went out the top of his shoulder blowing his shoulder joint to bits. His right arm was a useless rag. There was very little bleeding and he was conscious, but he couldn't move from the pain. Not that he had anywhere to go. He pulled the hood off his head with his other arm. He didn't care who saw him anymore.

CHAPTER FIFTEEN

Billy swung open the vault door and looked at the motley looking group staring up at him. The old man was propped up in the corner, staring at him from under his greasy faded baseball cap, with a look of utter contempt. The coffee can full of change was between his drawn up legs. The tops of one red sock and a black sock hung over his old work boots, on the end of his spindly legs.

Emma sat flat on the floor holding one of the kids on her lap, while the mother held the other one, now sitting beside Emma and crying silently with a sucker in her mouth. Neither one of them would look at Billy. The kids were eating candy and at least seemed to be occupied for the moment.

Ida sat in the other corner, with her arms crossed in front of her chest. Her nose appeared to be broken, and as she breathed little blood bubbles would form on the end of her nose. Dried blood was all over her white apron and her forearms. She looked mad and about to say something but thought better of it. Ida was a strong woman who worked hard and had had a tough life, and this punk was not going to ruin it now.

Jack and his son stood along the wall. When Billy came in Jack Jr. moved behind his father who gave him a disgusted look. Junior had been acting like a lowly coward in the face of this adversity.

Audrey sat by herself in the middle of the wall across from the Morton's, chewing on her cuticle and trying to keep her skirt wrapped tightly around her legs. She didn't appear to be afraid at all. She gave Billy a slight smile.

Billy was waving the gun in front of them, his face a sneer. "One of you set off the damn alarm. Who was it?" He snarled

For a second they were all very quiet and then Emma cleared her throat, but before she could say anything Jack Sr. said, "It was I."

The two men stood face to face.

"You were robbing my bank, what did you expect me to do?"

Billy seemed to be at a loss for words but he brought the pistol down hard on the side of Jack's head and he collapsed to his knees. Jack Jr. slid down the wall wailing and covered his head with his arms.

"Billy grabbed Jack Sr. by the hair and forced him back up. "If I don't get out of here in one piece, you're going to pay big time for this."

"Where's the other guy," Audrey asked, her head cocked to one side still chewing on her thumb.

For a second Billy just stared at her and then turning back to Jack Sr. said. "Oh yea, that other guy. You mean the traitor who tried to shoot me in the damn back, and got shot himself instead. He's upstairs lying on the floor." He pointed up the stairs behind him with the gun. He turned back to Audrey. "Why don't you, miss mouthy little girl and this old man, go get him and bring him down here. Yea, you do that right now and don't think about leaving this bank, cause if you do, I am going to kill the rest of your buddies and those kids over there." He pointed the gun at the young mother and her kids and she let out an anguished moan and tried to pull the kids closer to her.

Teddy heard footsteps coming from somewhere behind and thought it was Billy coming to finish him off but that was all right. He didn't deserve to live after what he had done. He was lying just in front of the swinging door that led around behind the tellers counter. He had thought about tying to get up and running out the front door but was afraid the cops would gun him down. That might be better however than Billy getting the satisfaction. He got up on his knees but he was dizzy and disoriented. He had to wait a second for his head to clear.

Jack had gone up first telling Audrey to stay low and behind him. "Those people outside have no idea who's good or bad, so just stay low and back of the counter," He had no idea if they were bringing a dead man, or a wounded one back down those stairs but right now he just knew, he better bring someone.

Jack pushed the door open while crouching behind it on his hands and knees. He was face to face with Teddy.

Even with the weight he had lost, there were no doubts to Jack, that this was his prodigal son, come home to rob his daddy's bank.

Jack did not know how he felt at that moment. Was it relief that Teddy was back, or fear and empathy for his wounds? Or was it anger and confusion that his son had participated in a robbery of his bank?

He turned behind him and told Audrey to wait for him at the top of the stairs and. she shrugged her shoulders and walked back.

Teddy spoke first. His voice was shaking and tears were running down his face. "Dad I never meant for this to happen. By the time I realized what was going on, it was too late."

"Teddy," Jack said while he examined his wounds. "Who shot you?"

"He did Dad."

"Why son?"

"Because I was trying to shoot him and stop this whole thing from happening."

Jack saw the rifle lying on the floor and reached over for it. Teddy realized his father was thinking about doing what he had failed to do and reached over with his good arm and grabbed his Dads hand. "Its empty Dad. He gave me an empty gun."

Jack brought his sons tearstained face to his chest and hugged him. "Well get through this Teddy. Well get through it. Let's get down stairs before he comes after us."

As soon as they were behind the tellers counter Jack help his son to his feet and with his arm around Teddy's back to steady him, they walked downstairs together.

When they walked into the vault Billy glared at Teddy but said nothing. Emma and Audrey, who knew the boy, let out a collective gasp. His brother looked at him as if he had seen a ghost.

Clem had tried to assess Barney's wound while still watching the front door. Barneys breathing seemed more labored and the puddle of blood under him had widened considerably. *How much blood can you lose and still live? Help better get here fast but when they do get here, how in the hell are they going to get Barney out of here without being in the line of fire themselves.* Two more cars passed behind him and now there were small crowds forming on the street corners oblivious to the danger they were in.

He keyed his radio again. "Kelly can you check on that ambulance and also would you call out the volunteer firemen. Tell them to block off all of the roads to this bank two blocks in each direction, and they are not to try coming into this area themselves. Where the hell is that other car with my backup?"

It was quiet for a moment and Clem used the time to try and see inside the bank again. *Damn it's getting hot out here. The tar is burning me right through my clothing. If that damn glass door wasn't so shot full of holes it would be easier to see inside. Maybe when help gets here we can sneak up there and bust the rest of the glass out.*

Barney, unconscious yet, let a long audible stream of gas loose. *Way to go big guy you just keep farting and breathing for me.* Clem reached over and squeezed Barneys leg.

"Clem this is Kelly do you read me?"

"Yea, go ahead."

"The ambulance just turned off on Parkers road and your other squad is still fifteen minutes off, but they told me to tell you their car is heating up so they can't push it any faster and they asked me, to ask you, if things were really that serious?"

"Oh for the love of Christ Kelly, have you been listening at all to what I have been telling you?" Clem was almost shouting in the radio. "Barney is shot and dying, and I'm pinned down in the street while the hot tar is burning welts on my ass, and they want to know if it is serious? Give me a damn break will you."

Just then the siren that called out the firefighters went off. This caused Adolph to stand partially up and say. "Is there a fire in the bank Clem?"

"No, and stay down. I just need some extra help."

Two men on the street corner, kitty corner from the bank hollered out to Clem. "Hey Sheriff is there anything we can do to help."

"Yes," Clem hollered back. "Get yourselves and everyone else the hell out of here."

What a bunch of dumb ass people. No wonder no one lives in this hick town. He saw the ambulance coming down the street in front of him and had no way to tell them not to get to close. Fortunately they were suspicious and stopped about a hundred feet away. Unfortunately they were running over to meet him.

"Wait" Clem holler at them. "There are people in there with guns." He pointed to the bank, and the two men squatted down in the street. "Turn your rig around and back it up to the front of this car. Stay as low as you can in the drivers seat and I will try and cover you." Many of the gathering spectators heard Clem and either went back into the cover of the stores, or fell back away from the area.

As the ambulance maneuvered back and forth in the street turning around, Clem got on his knees, his pistol pointing at the front door and watched over the back fender of the car. It seemed to be very quiet inside the bank and he had to wonder what was going on in there? *Had some mad man killed everyone? Who was in there when this whole thing started, and how many intruders where there? So many things to sort out, but first he needed to secure the scene and get Barney to a hospital. It was almost like they'd all disappeared somewhere. He had heard some muffled voices a few minuets back, but it was stone silent now.* One of the ambulance attendants was backing the rig down the side of the street right now and the other man was pushing a gurney, staying on the outside of the ambulance away from the door. He backed up until he hit the car shoving it back a few inches while Clem hollered. "Stop, Go the hell forward enough so you can get the doors opened."

"I'll cover you, he said to one of the men and you get him out of here." He pointed to Barney lying at his feet and then went back to staring at the banks front door.

They had left the gurney at its lowest position but still to lift Barney they would have to stand partially up, exposing themselves.

"You don't think those nuts are going to shoot at us," one of them asked. They were still crouching behind the ambulance.

Clem put his gun down on the lid of the trunk and duck walked around to Barneys head. Reaching down he grabbed him under the arms and pulled him over to the ambulance attendants. "Now get him out of here," he said sarcastically and retuned to his position at the back of the car. Down the street the fireman could be seen putting up barricades.

For now it was quiet in the vault. Billy was standing by the door looking angry and frustrated, going over his options, and watching over his group of very subdued hostages. There just weren't a lot of outs for him, in this mess that he could think of. First he needed to communicate somehow with the lawman outside, if he was going to strike some sort of compromise with them, without getting shot. There was no preplan for the pickle he was in now. When he had planed all of this so carefully, he had never thought it would come to this. He thought back to his army training and what had he been taught to do in this situation. He hadn't. It was name rank and serial number and that was all you told the enemy. The chapter of being holed up in a vault, with civilians you were robbing, had never come up.

Billy looked at Teddy sitting propped up against the wall with his fathers arm around him. Jack had been given some cloth bandages from Ida and was trying to tend to Teddy's wound as best he could. Jack seemed oblivious to what else was going on around him. Teddy had his eyes closed and his face was screwed up in pain. His fists were grabbing the folds of his trouser legs for support as Jack tied a bandage over the gaping hole in the top of his sons shoulder.

Teddy's brother had retreated to the other side and now sat by himself staring at the floor, and looking like someone had just run over his dog.

Audrey sat by herself chewing gum and nonchalantly watching Teddy as if this was some kind of a soap opera and she was just one of the players. The old man with his can of coins seemed to be calming down a little, his tremors that he had been experiencing had eased. He still clutched the coffee can between his legs and he still had said nothing to anybody.

Ida was busy using some of the smaller bits of cloth that she had torn from her apron and given to Jack for bandages, to stuff up her broken nose now and keep the bleeding at bay. Her eyes were swelling shut, and turning a black and blue color. She looked a little bit like a raccoon.

Emma was looking defiant and staring at Billy. He had no right to treat her or anybody else like this and she was contemplating how she was going to tell him just that. The gun and the violence he had already done was for now a deterrent, and none of them even knew about what he had done to Barney. She still held the younger of the two kids, a little girl about two, who had gone to sleep her tummy full of candy.

The mother of the kids was crying softly yet, as was her little boy about four who seemed content to rummage through his mothers handbag, sniffing his nose and just being a handful.

Almost as soon as the ambulance had left, the second squad pulled in steaming and smoking. Clem called them on the radio and asked one of them to come out where he was and the other one to relieve Adolph. Deputy Ron Webster a five-year veteran and one of Clem's better men dashed behind the Crown Victoria and squatted down next to Clem. "What we got Chief" he said.

"I got no idea Ron but it ain't good. As far as I know, right now there are one or two people in that bank with guns. They didn't come out nor did anyone else."

"Think there crazy enough to use them guns Clem?"

"Do I?-- No shit Ron, they shot Barney in the guts or didn't you pick up on that. You're standing in a puddle of his blood."

Ron looked own at the ground and moved over out of the gore. "We were so busy with the car Clem we didn't hear much of anything. Was Barney hurt bad?"

Yeah, I think he was hit pretty bad. But enough chit chat. You watch the front while I get out of here and try to figure out what the hell we are going to do." He looked over to where Adolph had been behind the trashcan. He was still there along with Cyrus Morton. Jack's cousin who was the other deputy. Clem ran to the corner of the bank building and hollered over to them. "Cyrus keep a close eye on them windows and Adolph you come with me." He indicated for Adolph to follow him and both men ran around to the storefront across the street from the bank where they could talk. "You got any idea who was in the bank when this happened Adolph?"

"Well That's Jack Jr. and Jack Sr.'s car out back. And I saw Emma Erickson out front unlocking the door this morning. There's a young girl that has been working there most days also. I think her name is Audrey Hall. Bud Halls oldest daughter. There might have been customers in there also, in fact I know that old man Martens was in there. I saw him go in when I was out front putting the awning down. I'm not sure who or how many others. It was early so don't think there were many."

Just then a woman in a white apron and bakers cap ran up to Clem talking hysterically. "Sheriff my mother was in that bank. What's going on?"

"Who's your Mother?" He asked.

"Ida Parsons. She owns the bakery right there." She pointed behind her.

Clem took the woman by the shoulders and looked her square in the eyes. "Look I don't know much right now but someone did try to rob the bank. As far as we know right now they are all still in there and so is everyone that was in the bank. As soon as I can I will be trying to get those people out of there, and getting those men into custody but you have to give me a few minutes and you have to stay away from here."

As soon as she left the Fire Chief came over and Clem met him. "Hi Chief," Clem said.

The Chief, Al Knurl's, and Clem knew each other well. They had been on many incidents together. "All I need is for your guys to keep everyone out of this area and get all of the people who are standing around gawking to leave also. Can you do that?"

"Sure Clem, we'll get right on that. Any idea how long this might last?"

"It won't be long if I have anything to say about it. Too damn hot to be screwing around like this." Clem wiped his brow with his shirt sleeve.

Dorothy Perkins was lounging in the over sized Jacuzzi tub in the hotel suite. She had a bloody Mary in her hand and could think of nothing else but Jack Morton lying between her legs today and tonight. He planed on being there by noon the last she had heard. She and Jack had sent each other so many conscious and subliminal messages over the last few weeks that her mind had worked her into a sexual frenzy. At her age that would be unusual for most women, but Dorothy had always been a sensual person and it had been a long, long time since she was last laid. He had been short with her last night and that worried her, but maybe a little wake up call was in order. Maybe if she told him what she was looking at right now it would prime the pump a little more. She looked down at her ample bosoms floating in the bubble bath and slid her hands over them, feeling the sensation through her nipples. She took another drink and then smiling seductively, dialed the bank in Morton. The phone gave a busy signal and that seemed odd. They had several lines and she had never had a busy signal before.

By eleven a.m Clem had several deputies in place at the bank and had scheduled a meeting with the Mayor, several people from the media, and the Fire chief in the basement of the Catholic church, where Father Bolton had given them a room to meet in. The initial reports back from the hospital were not good. Barney was in extremely critical condition. Clem had hoped to talk to him about what he had seen but it was not looking like that would happen.

He too had tried to call into the bank but the phones were off the hook. Somehow he was going to have to figure out, how he was going to communicate with these people. Right now though, he had something else to deal with and it was making him mad. The Mayor had demanded to see him, in this hastily set up meeting in the church basement behind the bank.

The Mayor, Thomas Stently seemed to be quite disturbed that something like this had taken place in his little town. "We need this resolved, and we need this resolved now Sheriff. Have you called the F.B.I? This is a federal offense you know. I know how the law reads when it comes to people robbing banks." He was tapping a pencil eraser on the table top as he talked with Clem and the pencil suddenly bounced off the table. He didn't retrieve it, he just kept staring at Clem his big old walrus mustache twitching like it had a mind of its own.

Clem sitting cross armed in a steel folding chair with St Michaels Church stenciled across the back looked at him skeptically. He had always felt the man was a pompous asshole and this only fortified his opinion. "Look Mayor with all due respect this whole incident is only a couple of hours old. We will call for help from other agencies when we need it. Right now I am not sure whom we are dealing with or who is still in that bank, but I assure you we will find out. I am not even sure if we even have a bank robbery. This could be someone with a grudge against the bank or someone who works there. This could be some nut case who the bank foreclosed on. Who the hell knows what's going on right now? Yes, I could call the F.B.I and the National Guard for that matter but I am not going to until I have more information." Turning to the Fire Chief before the Mayor could say anything in return Clem said, "Al I need your men to maintain a perimeter for me one block in each direction. No one comes in and everyone that is in there right now needs to get out. All stores need to close right now."

Al shook his head yes and said. "We will get right on that Clem".

Turning to the two media people from the local newspaper that the Mayor had drug over, Clem asked that they remain patient and stay out of the area. "You will be the first to know when I find out anything. Now if you excuse me, I need to try and resolve this whole mess."

"How do we get a hold of you Sheriff?" One of the reporters asked.

"You don't. I get a hold of you, and, now I have to get back to my men."

Just my luck Clem thought. *This needed to take place a block from the newspaper office. God damn jackals.*

The sheriff scooted low under the bank windows on the side of the building and made his way back to the front of the bank. Shielding his eyes from the blazing sun he squatted next to the blue Ford with Ron Webster. "Have you seen anything at all," he asked?

"No nothing. I don't think there is anybody on the main floor of the building. You sure they're people in there?"

"There in there all right." Clem lit a cigarette while he thought. "Ron some more help will be here soon. As soon as they get here, you and I are going to make our way into that bank. I have a feeling they're all downstairs."

CHAPTER SIXTEEN

Billy knew that it would only be a matter of time before they came in after him. He didn't want any gunplay but if it came to that-- then he was going to be ready. He had retrieved the rifle he gave to Teddy and had about a dozen shells in his pocket. It stood loaded now, next to the wall outside of the vault.

Both of the little kids were fussing now and getting on Billy's nerves. The old man had problems too and seemed to be having trouble breathing and Emma was concerned about him. She had loosened his collar but his wheezing was getting worse. "Why don't you let him go," she pleaded with Billy. "Can't you see he's sick? You don't need all of these people to accomplish, whatever sick thing it is you are trying to do. Let him and her and her kids go. She nodded at the young mother. Let Teddy go also, can't you see he is in a lot of pain, and needs medical attention. God knows how bad he's hurt." Emma had stood up and was looking defiant.

Billy walked over to her. "You shut the hell up old lady. I am in charge here and I will decide who goes and who stays. If anybody goes it will be me." He rubbed the pistol barrel under her nose, grabbed her hair and jerked her head back.

"I need to go to the bathroom," Audrey said behind him.

"Piss in your panties," Billy replied spinning around to face her and then just as quickly turned around again and asked Jack. "Is there a bathroom down here?"

"Yes it's down that hall," Jack indicated with a sweep of his arm to indicate where it was but said nothing more. He was sitting with his arm around Teddy. Neither one of them had said anything but the look they had for each other said that Jack had forgiven his son and Teddy was no

121

longer mad at his dad. Jack Jr. on the other hand, just sat across from them staring at both of them.

Billy walked over to Audrey. Go to the toilet little girl but don't shut that door. Wait a minute. Picking up the rifle he walked down the short hall and looked in the bathroom door. There were no windows in the room. Just a stool and a sink and some janitor's supplies stacked on some pine shelving. Across the hall from the bathroom was the break room and a box of pastries from Ida's bakery was on the tabletop. The phone on the wall caught his attention too and he went over intending to break it, but then thought better of it. He might need it himself. He took a jelly roll out of the box and wolfed it down on his way back to the vault.

"You can go now," he said to Audrey. "But get your little ass back here as soon as you're done. I'm watching you." He went over and sat down on the bottom step going upstairs, just in case she had some silly ideas.

He heard the toilet flush and then Audrey came back carrying a Dixie cup full of water which she gave to Teddy who had been asking for something to drink.

Billy had thought about hollering at her but right now he had enough problems so he let it pass. Maybe it was time to talk with the law and see if he could get some kind of a deal. Maybe the old gal was right and he should let some of them go, in exchange for favors of course. He went over and hung the phone in the vault back up so someone could call in if they wanted to. Maybe he would walk to the top of the stairs and see if he could figure out what was happening outside. He had been up there once when he retrieved the rifle but he hadn't looked around much. With all of his meticulous planning he had no idea right now how to handle this situation. But in the army, good soldiers never gave up and he would find a way, he was sure of that.

Clem had three more Deputies on the scene now, so he and Ron decided they would try to do some exploring. Main Street was deserted and all of the cars parked on the street had left but two. The one in front they presumed belonged to the crooks inside, and one other small green Chevy sedan could be from one of the hostages. Most of the shops had closed except the hardware store directly across the street from the bank where Adolph could be seen standing in the store front window, still with his shotgun held across his chest glaring at the front of the bank. He was mad that people would come into this town and do this, but he was angrier yet that he had been relieved of his duties. When Clem looked down the empty streets he could see the roadblocks at the end of each street and a few firemen standing by each barricade. He wiped his brow and looked at his watch. It was eleven thirty and it must be close to ninety degrees.

"Let's sneak up to the front door Ron, I'll pull it open, and then you watch the back of the room, and I will try and find some cover inside." Ron had a twelve gauge short barreled shot gun and Clem had his pearl handled thirty eight caliber colt revolver in his right hand. Clem took off, sliding up to the brick façade beside the front doors like he was stealing second base in a high school ball game. He peaked around the corner, pushed open the door so Ron could see inside. The place looked deserted. Squirming on his belly he crawled inside the door and hid partially behind some chairs that sat just inside.

"Make a dash for that desk," he whispered aloud to Ron and pointed to the same place where Ida had been filling out her deposit slip when Billy had come into the bank and sent her flying across the floor.

Ron held the weapon to his shoulder and bending over as far as he could and still move, started around the back of the blue ford.

The bullet from Billy's rifle went over Ron's head before he was even close to the door. So close that he felt the breeze part his hair as he fell flat to the pavement trying to crawl and hide behind the cement curb, lying in the pool of blood that had pooled there from Barney's wound. The remaining spider webbed glass fell out of the other door in a shower of fragments as the bullet went through it. The bullet then continued across the street, shattering the plate glass window Adolph was standing at and covering him with busted shards of glass. A cut opened up on the bridge of his nose but he did not move. He only growled like a mad Doberman. They had brought the battle to him now and no longer was he just an innocent bystander. He threw the shotgun to the floor and ran to the gun cabinet in the back of the store. His trembling hands selected a Remington model 742 Woods master, 30.06 deer rifle. He loaded the clip with shells and filled his pockets with more. Then going to the back of the store he pulled down a roof ladder and made his way to the roof. If they wanted a war then he would damn well give them a war.

Clem headed around the door and back outside, fully expecting to get shot in the back, but he was a sitting duck where he was. No more shots were fired and both Clem and Ron made it back to the safety of the car.

"Son of a bitch," Ron said. "That bastard means business."

Billy had retreated down the staircase after firing the rifle. Maybe now they would treat him seriously. Down in the vault, the others were eyeing the stairs and hoping the feet coming down the steps weren't Billy's. That somehow the law had taken him out and ended this whole ordeal. Their wishes were not to come true however, as Billy came back into view.

"Scared the shit out of those bastards," he gloated. He went over to the wall in the lunchroom and picked up the phone and dialed the emergency number.

"Sheriffs office," Kelly said. "Do you have an emergency?"

"Listen to me and listen good," Billy hissed into the phone. "I want those damn cops outside the front door to get away from my car so's I can drive away from here. If they try to follow me I will kill the woman I am taking with me. Do you understand?"

"Who is this?" Kelly asked.

"That's none of your goddamn business who I am, you just tell them cops what I said and right now."

Audrey was standing in the doorway of the vault and Billy shouted at her. "Get your ass back in there sweetheart."

Audrey smiled and retreated back into the vault.

Kelly was back on the line talking to him. "Are you the guy in the Morton Bank?"

"No I'm the Salvation Army. Who the hell do you think this is?" Billy was getting frustrated and he slammed the phone back in the receiver severing the connection and went back to the vault.

Clem's radios buzzed. It was Kelly. "Sheriff I just had some guy on the line who says he is inside the bank. You guys have a problem down there with someone in the bank?"

Clem looked at his radio. What a doorknob his dispatcher was. "Is he still on the line, Clem asked."

"Nope. He got mad and hung up."

He held his breath for moment and let it out softly. "Look Kelly try to get him back on the line and then patch me through to him."

"What's the number?"

"Damn it Kelly, look it up. I am lying in the middle of the street in front of the bank and it just so happens I went and forgot my damn phone book again."

Kelly looked at the mic in her hand and stuck out her tongue out at it. That sheriff could be a real smart ass sometimes.

Billy's eyes went from one hostage to the next as he took them all in. It was the first time he had really realized how many people he had down here. Audrey smiled at him when he looked at her. Billy scowled at her. *That little bitch needed to be knocked down a notch. She was getting too smart for her britches. Maybe he needed to take her britches off and teach her a lesson.*

He looked at Emma who sat passively holding one of the two children and staring in her lap. *She might be the one he took with him when he got out of this mess.* His gaze went to the young mother holding the other child, both of them sitting and crying. *I hate bawl babies like her. Remind me to give her something to bawl about before I leave.*

The old man-- he had to get rid of him. *He didn't know if he was acting or what, but he didn't look good. Besides he stunk and was making everybody sick.* His gaze went back to Jack Jr. who had moved off by himself in the corner, closest to Emma. *What a pathetic sack of shit. He should go over right now and kick him square in the nuts.*

Then there was Jack Sr. and Teddy, who right now was sleeping with his head in his Fathers lap. Some blood from his wound had leaked through his shirt and stained Jacks suit pants but he didn't seem to notice. His hand was intertwined in his son's hair and he sat back with his eyes closed.

Maybe he would let Teddy live. He wasn't sure yet. For now he wanted him to suffer a little.

The phone ringing brought him out of his little trance.

It was nearly noon and last night had been so special that Thelma thought she would go down to the bank and get Jack and take him out to lunch. Even though her sexual satisfaction last night had been utterly complete, she still felt like the game had only begun. They mustn't let this feeling every go away again.

She had showered and put on a flowery shirtwaist dress she knew Jack had never seen before. A touch of his favorite perfume high on her breasts and the second button left undone showed more than a hint of cleavage. Thelma looked in the mirror and giggled to herself. She hadn't had this much fun since before they were married.

The heat hit her like a warm oven as she went into the garage. She started the car and backed it out to let it cool down a bit. This car, unlike their past ones had air-conditioning.

Billy yanked the ringing receiver out of its cradle and yelled, "What do you want."

"I want you to walk out of the front door of this bank with your hands in the air. This is Sheriff Clem Nash talking and you have no way to escape, so you might as well pack it up, and if you have an accomplice they might as well do the same."

Clem thought for a moment. *Jezz that sounded pretty good. I hope to hell I was talking to the right person.*

"Well haughty taughty," Billy answered. "If it ain't the big bad sheriff talking like he was in charge here. Well let me tell you something sheriff. I'm in charge here and I'll tell you what the hell is going to happen. You and those other boys of yours should get the hell off the street, cause I am thinking about coming out and I will not be alone. You, can bet your little shiny tin badge on that. If anybody out there tries to stop me you will have one dead hostage to deal with. Maybe more. Maybe I'll bring them all along."

Clem had to stop and think for a second. This guy was making him extremely angry but if somebody got killed, he would be in deep trouble. "Listen to me," Clem said. "Let those people go and then you and I can sit down and come to some kind of an agreement here, huh?"

"I might let one of them go Billy said. Just to show you my hearts in the right place." He hung up the phone.

Billy walked over to the old man, and staring down at him kicked him in the bottom of his ragged shoe. "You, take your shit and your decrypt wrinkled ass and get out of here. You're stinking up the place anyway.

Here's a little something for your trouble. Billy reached in to the duffle bag Jack had stuffed the bills into and brought out a bundle of twenties. "Get yourself some new clothes and shoes. Maybe some socks that match. Maybe buy yourself a shower too while you're at it." Billy held out his hand and pulled the old man up. Then he wiped his hand on his pants as if he had just touched something bad. All of the others just watched and said nothing. "Now get going and don't tell that sheriff anything because if you do when I get out of here-- and I will-- I will hunt you down and kill ya."

The old man said nothing but started out of the vault and up the stairs one step at a time.

"You want me to him call back?" Kelly asked Clem over the radio realizing the connection had been lost.

"No I need to think about this for a while Kelly. I'll let you know." He looked around him. It was getting damn hot out. The sun was cooking him and Ron, and he just wanted to get this thing over with and get back to his office. He looked down the street and some woman was running in his direction with two firemen chasing her. *Who the hell could this be? Not another damn newspaper person. I better go meet her before she gets too close.*

CHAPTER SEVENTEEN

Thelma stopped short in her tracks when she saw the Sheriff coming towards her. The fireman who had tried to restrain her told her that some crazy person was holed up in the bank. She had run right by him screaming and would have no part in being restrained by him or anybody else. As she got closer, Clem recognized that this was Thelma Morton. He remembered her from the night he and Barney had stopped by to talk to her about her missing teenage son.

"Where's my son and my husband Sheriff? Are they still in there?"

Clem had intercepted her with a bear hug to make her stay where she was. He couldn't help thinking she smelled very nice on this hot sticky day. "Now Mrs. Morton you need to settle down. I really can't tell you a lot, but as far as I know two men tried to hold up the bank this morning. My deputy surprised them and now they have several people held hostage." He didn't mention they had shot Barney, not wanting to upset her more than she already was.

Thelma lunged against him but he held her tight. "I am not going to release you until you promise me you will stay right here and listen to what I have to say. You run down there and upset the apple cart-- somebody just might get shot."

Thelma quit resisting Clem and started sobbing instead, buring her face in Clem's broad shoulder. It just too much Sheriff," she wailed. "First my son Teddy disappears and I have no idea where he is, and now my husband and my older son are being held against their will and you and your men are out here in the street instead of going in there and freeing those people. I can't take much more of this." She looked up at Clem, her eyes pleading for him to do something. Tears were running down her face, making muddy rivulets out of her mascara. "Do something for a change," she screamed her fists balled up, grabbing his uniform shirt and pulling it away from his body.

"Look Mrs. Morton. These people have already shot one person and maybe more, and for us to rush in there--- Clem held his hands out wide in desperation of what else to say. "Well it just might end up in a blood bath that no one wants to see happen. Most of the time these things are resolved by negotiations and no one gets hurt. I prefer to try that, don't you?"

Thelma didn't answer him, as she was busy digging in her bag for her tissues. Clem still stood in her way in case she was going to try an end around on him, but she seemed to be content for the time being.

"Clem" Ron hollered. "Someone is coming out."

"Go back to the barricades and I will come and see you in a few minutes." He gave her a small shove towards the end of the street she had come from. For a moment she hesitated, but then started walking back.

Content that she was leaving, Clem turned his attention to where Ron stood in back of the car, his pistol griped in both hands, trained on an old man who seemed totally bewildered as he walked out of the bank, his shuffling feet crunching in the broken glass. Held tight in his shaking hands was a red coffee can that was making jingling noises from the vibrations. He was squinting in the bright sunlight but hadn't said anything.

Clem meanwhile, with his attention seemingly focused on the scene playing out in front of the bank, caught some movement high on the roof of the building across the street and he was awe struck by what he saw. It was Adolph and he was aiming a rifle straight at the two men across the street. Clem broke into a run and pointing up at Adolph screamed. "Get down of that roof, you son of a bitch. This ain't no goddamn war game Adolph, and you were told to clear out of the area. Now go before I come up there and tie your ass to your flag pole," he shouted.

Adolph ducked down below the parapet, but he didn't leave the roof. *This is my property and no tin badge sheriff is going to tell me I can't guard it. They already shot at me and broke out a three hundred dollar window. If anybody wants me out of here they are going to have to remove me. If he comes up here I'll tie his ass to the flagpole.*

He clicked the safety back on the rifle and taking off his bandana wiped the sweat from his brow. This could be a long day but any soldier, who had been on Pork Chop Hill, knew how to handle a long day.

Billy had walked down to the lunchroom keeping a vigilant eye on the open vault door. He picked up the box with the bakery goods and walked back to the vault. "Anybody hungry," he said. "You all better eat up, cause its going to be a long day."

Right now he sensed that no one had any advantage here and that he was going to have to procure his freedom somehow with some kind of a deal. He was not going to contact them; they could just call him when they got damn good and ready. If this thing drug out to long maybe he would have to lock the hostages in the vault. Sooner or later he was going to get sleepy. Those cops outside were not going to get sleepy however and maybe he would get caught if he let his guard down. *Damn that Teddy why the hell did he have to be a turncoat? If they had stuck together, ain't no one was gonna sneak in on them but now all by himself?*

Billy walked back out of the vault and listened for noises upstairs. Maybe he would sneak up there and take another look. At the top of the stairs across the hall was the alarm panel and it was blinking red with a trouble light illuminated. He stopped to look at it and noticed that it had three zones numbered one, two and three. Zone one showed that it was in default whatever that meant. The other two zones were normal. He raced back down the stairs and motioned for Jack Sr. to come with him.

"Tell me about this alarm system," he asked Jack.

"What do you want to know," Jack answered.

"Why is that light blinking on one zone and not the others?"

"Jack took his glasses out of his coat pocket and looked carefully at the alarm panel. "Well it's blinking because I set off the silent alarm when you came in. The other two zones are motion detectors and they weren't on. We always shut them off the first thing in the morning."

Billy stared at Jack. "Where are the detectors that sense the motion?"

"By the front and back door. Another one watches that set of windows along the side of the building. Anyone coming in is going to set them off. You can't get around them."

"If you turn this on, will they work?"

"As long as whoever sets them off is upstairs they will. You have thirty seconds to leave either upstairs or outside once you turn them on."

Billy looked at Jack with a sinister smile spreading across his face. "Turn it on Mr. Morton and let's get downstairs shall we."

Clem had taken the old man down the street and had him in the back seat of a squad car. The man appeared to be bewildered and in a state of confusion. When Clem asked who he was, he just stared at him with vacant eyes that said I want to go home, so just leave me alone. Clem took his wallet from him and in it was a driver's license that had been expired for seven years. It said his name was William O. Bradford and he lived at 734 Fox Lane. He was eighty-nine years old.

Clem walked back down to Ron leaving the old man locked in the back of the car. "I'm not sure we're going to get any information out of this guy. He is about three heartbeats away from taking the leap to the next world. Maybe if I get him home and in his own house he will wake up a little. It's worth a try."

It felt good to get out of the street and away from the scene. Maybe it would also help him clear his thoughts and make a right decision on where he was going with all of this.

Fox Lane was a gravel road not much wider than an alley. There was only one house on it and it looked unfit for human habitation. It was an old two-story house with wooden shingles that had turned gray with age, covered with green moss. The house was obscured with a heavy cover of leafy vines that covered the faded out white clapboard siding. The red brick chimney was missing several bricks from the top of it; one of the bricks still lay on the roof.

Clem stopped and walked around to the back to let the old man out. He was sitting with the coffee can still cradled between his legs. The bundle of bills was lying on the bottom of the can, on top of the coins. Clem reached in the can to take the bills out, but the old man grabbed his wrist. "Easy fellow. I just wanted to see what you had here. I'm not going to take it away from you." They were all brand new twenties wrapped with a paper band.

"Where did you get these?" Clem asked.

The old man looked at him and shrugged his shoulders.

Clem looked at the bills and then threw them back into the can. He would deal with that later.

The back door creaked as Clem pushed it open and then a wave of hot mustiness washed over him as he stepped inside. The house was packed with boxes and junk as far as the eye could see. The old man walked to an old enamel sink and drew a glass of water in a dirty glass. He drank slowly' looking out a small kitchen window that was so filthy it was like looking through wax paper.

"Can you tell me who's still in the bank?" Clem asked

He turned slowly, looking so weary Clem thought he would wither and die on the spot. "Nine people" he said. "I don't know any of them except Ida."

"Ida from the bakery?" Clem asked

He nodded his head slowly yes, and ran his hand through his snow-white greasy hair. He wasn't shaking anymore.

"How many robbers are there?"

"Two." He turned and drew another glass of water. "One of them is shot in the arm."

Had Barney got one of them?

"Look I know you been through a lot today so I'm going to leave and let you rest, but maybe I'll be back to talk to you later. Would that be alright?"

He sat down in a chipped up red painted enamel chair with a couple of spindles missing out of the back. "I'll be here," he said.

Clem looked at his watch as he drove back to the bank. It was nearly three o'clock. Maybe he should get some fresh men into place and then he would try to talk to this nut in the bank once more. This crap had gone on long enough.

Billy was sitting on the floor of the vault with the rest of them. He felt pretty good about using the alarm system to his own advantage. Now he had some help with security. *To hell with Teddy, he could die for all he cared.*

He looked across the vault at Audrey who was twirling her long brown hair around her fingers. She didn't seem to be very upset about all of this.

She smiled at Billy realizing he was looking at her, but didn't say anything to him. She had a plan but she had to wait for the time to be right.

Emma was a different case. If looks could kill Billy would be dead in his tracks, and right now she looked like she was ready to give him another one of her speeches. This was one person, he almost feared. He had to keep her in line that was for sure.

Ida was bent over with her head in her lap. She refused to have anything to say to anybody.

The young mother had gone with her kids to the bathroom. The kids seemed to be quiet for the time being. She had eyed the stairs when she walked out of the vault but then turned and looked at Billy watching her and thought better of it. Now she came back and took her place on the floor again. "Please let me and my kids go," she said. "We're no good to you and the kids need diapers. The youngest one needs some medicine she was supposed to take an hour ago."

Billy stared at her. "You shut up," he said.

Maybe I should let the kids go, but she is staying put. Besides she's kind of cute. Maybe what she needs is little bit of what Billy has to offer. He smiled at the thought of doing it with her on the lunchroom table.

Jack Jr. was in the corner, his face turned to the wall, His hands drawn up inside his sleeves and his arms crossed. His Father sat beside him holding Teddy to his other side. A small puddle of blood had dripped off Teddy's arm onto the floor. Teddy's face was turned to the wall.

"He needs a Doctor." Jack said.

"Call one," Billy answered. "If you can get him to make a house call, then fine, but Teddy ain't going anywhere until I do." The phone rang again.

Dorothy Perkins was getting angrier by the minute. Jack was supposed to be here by noon and now it was going on four and he was nowhere to be found. She pushed her glass back on the hotel bar. She had had enough to drink for now. If Jack was not here by six she was checking out. Maybe she was being hasty and there was an explanation for his absence. Taking her purse she headed back to her room.

On the bed was the white peignoir that she bought for tonight. She had put it on this morning and arranged the lighting so when she walked around Jack would see just enough of Dorothy through the filmy clothe to make him go for a home run.

She dialed the bank. The phone rang several times before some man picked it up and said, "What do you want."

"I want to talk to Jack Morton," Dorothy said. "You need some manners sir."

Billy laughed while he held the phone out away from his ear. "Listen baby I don't know who you are and care less but Jack Morton is busy right now so piss off." He slammed the phone down.

Clem met once more with the mayor and fire chief after assuring Thelma that everything that could be done was being done. She seemed to understand but didn't leave the barricade this time, staying behind it. He told them, "that this thing was not going to be easily resolved and right now he was bringing in some fresh deputies. There would be no attempt to rush the bank. Not today anyway."

Another man who had stayed behind the barricade waited his turn to talk to the sheriff and introduced himself as Doug Waters. He had come home from work to find his wife and kids missing and right now he was sure she was in the bank.

"That's her car parked just down from the bank and she told me this morning before I left for work she was going there to cash in some bonds." Doug was a diminutive man. He had dark black hair he wore in a crew cut and looked as if he would be lucky to weigh one hundred and ten pounds and be five feet four. He came to the middle of Clem's chest.

"Hang on a minute," Clem said, "I want to talk to you more." He turned back to the Mayor. "Why don't we talk to the good Padre over at St Michaels and see if we can use that room we were in this morning for a kind of command center of sorts. That would be much better then discussing this here in the street. Too many ears out here right now."

As for Doug Waters he too had shown some faith in the Sheriffs tactics, so he took his place along side of Thelma, behind the barricade maintaining a vigil.

Clem's plan right now was to try and talk to the robber in the bank once more, and reach some kind of a compromise. Otherwise they were just going to wait him out. He had a good idea now who was in the bank with the two robbers. He had no idea what they wanted to stop this whole thing-- but he aimed to find out. He called Kelly on the radio and said "Patch me through to the bank again, if you can."

Billy looked at the ringing phone again. This better not be some other crackpot or he was going to tear this phone out of the wall for good.

CHAPTER EIGHTEEN

"What do you want?" Billy asked sarcastically

"No, I want to know what it is you want?" Clem asked. "Look I'm not in the habit of making deals with petty crooks, but if there is some way we can settle this quietly with out anyone getting hurt than I'm open to talking about it."

"I'm going to sleep on it Sheriff, because it's too late in the day to do anything now, but there is one thing I want. That is for you to get us all some grub and I need a case of good beer."

"How many are you?" Clem asked. He knew the answer but just wanted Billy to confirm it. Settling down for the night was probably a good idea. Maybe cooler heads would prevail in the morning. He did need to get some concession from him however if he was going to get them some food.

"I can get you food, but no beer and what's in it for me if I do feed you all?" "Everybody stays alive sheriff. How's that for starters?" Billy scratched his head. *Maybe now would be a good time to get rid of those crying kids. They were driving him nuts."*

"Here's the deal sheriff. I am going to send out the two little kids. But that's all, and that's the end of letting people go. You understand me?"

Clem was seething. This goddamn redneck bastard was calling the shots on him but right now he had no choice. "Send the kids out and I will send some food in.?"

He dropped the phone so it was hanging by the cord, not breaking the connection.

Slowly he swaggered over to the to the young mother. "The kids are being released. Her eyes widened and she pointed to her chest with her forefinger.

"Not you stupid. Just your kids."

He turned to Jack Jr. "You know how to shut that alarm off cowboy." Young Jack shook his head yes. Then you take these kids to the top of the stairs and shut off the alarm. Then walk them to the front door but listen closely to me now. He grabbed him by the throat to emphasize his point. I will be watching you and if you try to go out that door with those kids I will shoot you right in the back of the head. He poked the rifle barrel in Jack Jr.'s chest. "Tell me what I just told you."

Jack Jr. repeated Billy's words to the best of his memory.

"Why won't you let her go with the kids?" Emma asked Billy from behind him. She was standing back up with her hands on her hips in an authoritarian pose. Billy spun around and now shoved the rifle in the middle of Emma's chest. "I told you once old lady to shut the hell up. Now what part of that didn't you understand?" His teeth were clenched and he talked from behind them in an exaggerated whisper. I ought to blow your baggy tits off, that's what I ought to do." Emma sunk back down to the floor her arms folded across her chest and clutched her bodice.

Jack Jr. had stood up and was picking up the smallest child from the Mother's arms. It was crying hard and reaching back for its mother who was also sobbing.

"You kids go with the nice man. He is going to take you to Daddy," she said, talking between sobs to the older child. Billy motioned for them to go and then followed them up the stairs a few step behind them, but not before he picked the phone back up and said, "they're coming out Sheriff. Call me back when they're outside." He hung the phone back up.

At the top of the stairs Jack Jr. went to the alarm panel and punched in some code and the indicator lights went out. Then taking the crying kids hands he walked around the tellers counter and headed for the main entrance. Billy racked the weapon from behind the counter and said. "You're in my sights bastard. Don't forget that."

Ron and Clem saw the people coming out through the bank and didn't know what to think of it. He clicked the safety off on his gun. "Easy," Clem whispered. "Watch them but be careful with the kids there."

When they reached the busted door, Jack Jr. set the little one down and then gave his older brother his tiny hand. He pointed at Ron and showed them where to walk to him. He hesitated for a second as if to turn and come back, but then in one quick motion he dove out the door and getting to his feet sprinted down the street straight at Thelma.

Billy squatting behind the tellers counter had no time to react. Had he shot he risked hitting the kids. "Your old man is dead meat he screamed and ran back down the stairs through the door of the vault and hit Jack Sr. in the head with the butt of the rifle. He slumped backward unconscious, blood flowing from a cut on his forehead. Teddy tried to stand, but Billy kicked his feet back out from under him. He was so mad he was literally snarling now. Even Audrey shrunk down as small as she could make herself and would not make eye contact with him.

The phone rang again and it was Clem. "Look I sent someone to get you food and drinks so just settle down. I don't want anyone hurt."

"You send that bastard back in here or I am going to blow his old mans brains all over the rest of these people. That chicken shit don't deserve to live for what he just done."

Clem could tell from Billy's voice that this irrational man had become even more angry and agitated. He looked up the street and saw Jack Jr. wrapped in his mothers embrace. This was just another thing gone wrong and he had no idea how to fix it.

"I will talk with him but there is no way I can make him go back in there to you if he doesn't want to."

The phone was silent but he could tell by the back ground noise the line was still open. Then he heard a click and the connection was lost.

"Ron. Go get one of the guys to go to a restaurant and get enough food for a half a dozen people. Have them put it in a box and put a couple of beers in there also."

"You nuts Clem? You're going to give that goofball beer? As if he ain't screwy enough already?"

"Just get the food coming Ron and leave that to me." He sat down in the street with his back to the car. A shadow moved on the roof of the hardware store. *That damn Adolph was still up there. As soon as Ron came back with the food he was going to go over there and arrest him. Enough was enough.*

The sun had set behind the buildings and it was cooling down somewhat. He reached in his pants pocket for his pocket watch. It was seven thirty. Fresh troops would be here soon. Maybe he needed to just let this whole thing settle down for a while. He was getting weary and it was hard to think right now.

Clem keyed his hand held radio. "Cyrus you still here?"

"Right around the corner Clem." The call on the radio had surprised him as he had been sitting there behind the trash container for hours with no idea what was going on.

"Get somebody to relieve you, and then do me a favor. Find the druggist from the pharmacy that's next to the bank here. Tell him to come down to his store. I want to talk to him. Also get a hold of that jerk that ran down the street here a few minutes ago and take him and his mother over to the Church and keep them there. I want to talk with him. Right now he's still down the street by the barricade where he ran, hugging the crap out of his Mother. I can see him from here"

Clems plan for now was just to secure the scene. He would leave the food in the middle of the bank and then he was going to go over and talk to Jack Jr. The robber would drink his drugged up beer and if all went well, fall asleep. The beer was the only thing he could be reasonably assured that only he would drink. That is if the druggist showed up. Clem also thought about talking to Doug Waters the father of the two children but he had swept up his kids and left the scene. He would look for them later.

Ben Gerard the local druggist did show up, and he was mad because his business was shut off. "Why the hell don't you go in and get this crackpot Sheriff and let this town get back to its business. Do you know how much business I lost today, and there are people who need their medicine's." The old druggist looked like a wild man and was living up to his image. He was of average height and weight, with thick black bushy eyebrows that seemed to hang over a rather prominent nose. He still had on his white lab coat and a red tie.

Clem stood in front of the drug store, leaning against the storefront with his arms crossed across his chest, letting Ben rant on. Another officer had taken up his vigil in front of the bank and seemed to be amused by the exchange.

"Look Ben. You have every right to be mad, but if you will just listen to me for a second, maybe you can help us bring this thing to a timely close. I'm not happy about this situation either. There are a million things I would rather be doing then standing here talking to you right now, or should I say listening to you." Clem was nose to nose with him now. The sheriffs' statement had set Ben back a little and now he looked as if his feelings had been hurt. He fumbled with his tie as he listened sheepishly.

"Look do you have some kind of a sedative I can put in some food or drink that will make this guy go to sleep?"

"What do you mean a sleeping pill?"

"Sleeping pill, tranquilizer I don't care; just so it knocks him out so we can go in there and put him in cuffs. He has a gun and has already used it, so you have to understand the gravity of the situation here."

Ron pulled up with the food in a brown cardboard box. It smelled like fried Chicken and made Clem realize he had not eaten all day. "Set it down Ron, call it a day and go home. I'll l talk to you tomorrow." Ron was more than happy to leave. It had been a long day.

Ben had gone into the store and now he came out with a brown bottle that was filled with some white powder.

"This stuff will do the trick Sheriff. Any idea how big this guy is?"

Clem shook his head and smiled. "Why don't' you just dole out a dose for an average man Ben. How the hell should I know how big the guy is?"

Ben reached in his pocket in his lab coat and took out a gelatin capsule. He proceeded to fill it and handed it to the sheriff.

"Think he could taste this stuff if I put it in a can of beer the sheriff asked?"

"I doubt it. You're giving this nut beer?"

"That's what he asked for. Two cans shouldn't make him that squirrelly."

Clem took out his key ring and unfolded the church key that was on the ring and popped open the two cans of beer. He put half of the contents of the capsule in each can and then reaching for the radio on his belt, he called the dispatcher.

Kelly had gone home and was replaced by the night dispatcher who was named Sharon. "Sharon give me that phone number Kelly was getting through at the bank today." He could hear some papers shuffling and then she came back with the number.

Ben Gerard was still standing in front of the drug store. "Need to use your phone before you lock up," Clem said.

It took six rings before Billy answered with his usual, "What do you want?"

"I have some food for you guys," said Clem." I'm going to walk in the bank and leave it on the tellers counter in the back. I will be unarmed and alone and if you want to talk this over, this might be a good time to do it."

"Just bring the food, and then get out."

He had never in all of his years as a Deputy and Sheriff felt more vulnerable than he did right now. He had left his gun belt with the Deputy behind the car. There had been a brief thought about sticking his revolver in the back of his pants but then he thought. *If have to turn and walk out of there and if he saw it--- well. This guy is mad enough right now; there is no sense in adding any fuel to the fire.*

The broken glass from the door crunched under his boots. He passed the congealed puddle of blood from Barney on the way in that was now being ingested by flies in the hot summer night. *He should call and find out how he was doing. To damn many things to think about right now. Here is more blood on the floor by the kiosk right inside the door. Who does that belong to?*

It was deathly quiet in the bank. Just the tick, tick, tick, of a clock high on the wall in the back. All of the lights upstairs had been shut off, but there was light coming from the light in the back of the bank by the downstairs steps. *Was he up here watching me? More blood on the floor here by the tellers counter. How many people were hurt in here? This is nuts.*

Clem set the box of food on the counter and waited for a second. *Should I call out for him? No if he wanted to talk he would be here. Best to let things settle down a little.* He turned and traced his steps back out.

Clem stopped at the car out front to get his gun belt back. He gave the deputy some last second instructions and then walked around the corner heading for the church. He had to talk to Jack Jr. and he hoped he would be there. *To hell with Adolph. If he wanted to sit on the roof of his store in the heat let him. I got enough damn nuts to deal with. I need to call Doree also and tell her I won't be home tonight and to bring me some fresh clothes for tomorrow.* He thought of his wife of twenty-five years sitting home waiting for him. She was going to be mad at him again as usual. He could hear it now.

"Clem I have been playing second fiddle to that job of yours for most of our married life. One of these days you are going to come home and I will be gone. Your kids never got to know you and neither did I."

He stopped short by the back door of the church. Downstairs some women were setting up tables and chairs in the hall where they had met this morning. It was bingo night. Maybe no one was here. Maybe he should go see the good Father and see if they could still use the place. He walked across the drive to the parish house. Father Bolton was just coming out.

"Evening Father."

"Sheriff. How are things going over there?" He nodded his head at the bank building.

"Not real good. Say Father is it still all right if we use the room in the basement for a meeting. This whole thing is getting more complicated by the minute."

"Sure thing. Bingo tonight you know, but there are a few classrooms down there they won't be using so just pick one out and help yourself. Shut off the lights when you're done."

He walked around to the front to see if Ron was out there with Mrs. Morton and Jack Jr. They were all sitting on the front steps. "Let's go around to the back he said to Thelma and Jack Jr. Father Bolton says we can use a room downstairs to talk in. Ron you can take off now."

Billy sat the food in the middle of the floor and told them to help themselves. He had taken the two cans of beer out of the box and had one in each hand eyeing them suspiciously. Something stunk here. Why would he give him beer when he said empathically that he wouldn't and why would he open the cans for him? He sniffed through the triangle openings on the can tops. It smelled like beer and the refreshing smell coupled with the coolness of the cans was making it hard to not throw caution to the winds and chug one down. Maybe he would be happy with one beer and make someone else drink one of them as a test. But maybe only one can was tinkered with, if it was and which one was it?

He went into the lunch room and looking around found just what he was looking for. An empty water pitcher. He poured both cans in the picture and watched the heady foam for any signs of foreign substances. Seeing none he went back to the vault with a glass and stood in front of

Emma who was eating a piece of chicken and a biscuit. He filled the glass and told her. "Drink this woman."

"Why," she said. "I'm fine with some water."

Billy grabbed her hair and slammed her head against the wall. "Drink it or I will pour it down your damn throat."

Emma quickly guzzled the beer and handed him the glass. *What the heck was the big deal about that?*" she thought.

Billy sat down and ate a biscuit himself. Everybody had eaten but Ida, who still sat quietly, picking dried blood out of her nose and staring at the floor.

To hell with her he thought. *She don't want to eat, she don't have too. Stubborn old cow.*

"Go turn that alarm system back on," he said to Jack Morton who was now conscious but slightly unsteady on his feet. He held onto the wall with both hands as he went and did as Billy had asked. When Jack came back down Billy waited about a half an hour. Then seeing Emma sleeping on the floor, Billy poured the rest of the beer down the floor drain and closed the vault door. He sat down outside the vault door leaning against it. It was time to call it a day. *Tomorrow was going to be another story and this sheriff was going to regret messing with Billy Joe Stanton.*

CHAPTER NINETEEN

Clem listened closely as Jack Jr. told him about Teddy and Billy. He had few facts to tell, but his perception was that the two of them had a plan to rob the bank and then had a falling out and Billy shot him.

Right now he said, Teddy seemed dazed and unresponsive, clinging to his father. His injuries could or could not be responsible for his lethargic condition. It also could be the shame of it all.

Thelma listened closely as her oldest son talked. Yes, Jack and Teddy were being held hostage by some fanatical man, but right now at least she knew where Teddy was and Jack had done a good job of assuring his Mother that Teddy's injuries were not life threatening. She would deal with what he had done when the time came. Not now.

Ida was also suffering and Jack Jr. suspected she had suffered a concussion. His father who had cooperated with Billy as best he could was fine and so were Emma, Audrey and Debra Fisher.

"Did you not hear what he shouted at you when you made your escape?" Clem asked.

Jack did not answer him preferring to stare at the floor and pick lint of his trouser legs.

"Do you think he might carry out that threat?"

Jack shrugged his shoulders. He had no answers and knew he was being depicted as a coward in front of his mother.

The sheriff was too tired and confused to carry on with this any longer and so he walked outside and stood in the alley thinking to himself. *What if the sedative had worked? How would he know and was it worth the risk to try and go in and find out? But if Billy did fall asleep wouldn't the hostages come out? That is if they could. He needed to get some rest. Maybe if he laid down somewhere for just a few hours,* but just then Al Kruls the Fire Chief walked around the corner of the bank and approached him.

"How much longer is this going to go on Sheriff? My men are tried and want to go home."

Clem looked at him with disdain. "They will be replaced by Deputies in the morning he said. Thanks for the help," he said sarcastically. He walked over to his squad car still parked up against the back door of the bank and crawled in the back seat and laid down. "If anyone needs me I will be in my car," he radioed the deputy in front of the bank.

"Right Sheriff," he answered and "oh by the way, I heard Barney is hanging in there. He's not out of the woods yet but its looking better."

"Thanks," Clem answered.

Dorothy Perkins calls to Jack's phone both at home and work had gone unanswered. She packed her bags and left the hotel in a huff. She was going back to Morton, tomorrow morning she was going to draw out all of her funds from Jacks bank and give him a much-needed piece of her mind instead of the piece of her she had fantasized him taking. She was insulted and defiant. No one treated Dorothy Perkins like this and got away with it. Not even the great Jack Morton.

Billy had let them all visit the bathroom and then told them to go to sleep. They were not going home anytime soon as far as he was concerned. He took up his vigil out side of the vaults closed door, and dozed on and off with the rifle in his lap, content that the alarm system would warn him of any intruders. Inside the vault Jack was getting more and more concerned about Teddy. He seemed to have a high fever and his arm from the wound on down was turning a bluish black. He was also concerned about Ida. She still had not eaten or drank that he knew of, or gone to the bathroom. He had tried to talk to her but she only looked at him with a confused face, as if she wasn't aware of what was going on.

Soon after leaving the church basement and lying down in the back seat of the car, Doree showed up at the scene and was escorted to Clem's car. She rapped softly on the window with her wedding ring. *It was good for something,* she thought. He hadn't been sleeping and seeing her face in the streetlight behind the bank he quickly sat up and unlocked the door. She had a clean uniform and underwear in a brown paper bag.

"I got your message and brought you some clothes," she said softly.

"I'm really sorry about this," Clem tried to explain but she shushed him.

"I watch the news," she said.

"It's on the news?"

"It's on the television news and the radio. There are a lot of people out there that don't agree with your strategy Clem. They're making you look foolish, and I'm not so sure I totally disagree with them. She sat an arm length away from him holding her mouth in a pout. "You have a family that needs you Clem. You don't have to be here and you know that. There are people who work for you that can do the job very well. You're married to me Clement not that damn sheriff's office."

Clem did not answer her. They had had this discussion so many times before and it never ended well.

"It will be over in the morning. One way or the other."

"So the sheriff does have a plan."

Once again he did not answer her. He had no plan and was stalling for time.

"How are the kids?"

"Lonely for their father," she spit back at him.

"Look Doree, there are people down there in that bank basement that are fighting for their lives, and I for one want to see they make it out alive."

"Well you have a family that is fighting too Clem. Fighting for attention from a husband and a father." The door was still unlatched and her hand had never left the lever from the moment she sat down. Now she hastily slid forward and stepped out in one motion. "Call me if you can." She was crying and knew that she had better leave before she made a spectacle out of herself.

Clem slammed his fist into the back of the seat in front of him. That bastard down there was going down tomorrow. He had better get thinking how he was going to do it and quickly.

When the sun in a blue cloudless sky finally peeked over the top of the buildings, Clem had slept little if at all. He had however made a plan, One more time he would try to meet face to face with this maniac, and if that failed, then they were going to resort to tear gas, and if that failed, then he would call in the F.B.I. and go home to Doree and the kids, content in his mind that he had done all that he could.

He took his clean clothes and went over to the church. Lights were on downstairs and some women were making coffee already. Father Bolton in an unusually benevolent mood had called them and asked them to provide food and drinks for the officers.

Clem retreated to the bathroom, washed his face and hands and then changed. He looked into the mirror at a man who was not only weary, but also downright haggard. He splashed some cold water on his face, wiped it dry and went out to face the music.

The two women smiled and asked what he wanted to eat. Clem putting on a good face said "Maybe in a little bit. I'll just have some coffee for now." Two of the volunteer firefighters that were handling the barricades were eating eggs and sausages at a small table. Clem nodded to them but they hardly seemed to notice him. He had to get to a phone. In a small room off the kitchen he found what he needed. It was six thirty and Ron would be leaving the office soon.

"Morning Sheriff," Ron said. "What's the game plan today?"

"Well a couple of things Ron, before you come down here. We need to take over these barricades so bring at least four more men in then we had yesterday. I also want you to bring a case of tear gas canisters and some masks. Some fresh batteries for my hand held, and pickup breakfast for the hostages. Also call the electric company and have them standby to cut the power to the building. Got all that?"

"Got it Clem and we'll be there in an hour."

He stepped outside right in the face of a couple of reporters.

Clem answered their question as best he could for a few minutes, but then said, "he had to leave" and fled back into the church until they left.

Teddy was running a high fever this morning and Jack was more than a little concerned.

"Look, why don't you let Teddy and Irma go? They are both hurt and need medical attention. How many people do you need? The more there is of us, the more you have to watch." They were standing outside of the vault door while most of the others were using the bathroom. All except Irma who had soiled herself during the night time and still refused attention from anyone.

"I told you when we let those kids go that no one else was leaving and I meant it." Billy was staring at Jack through blood shot eyes. Even though the alarm system had been on, he had not slept. "Now get the hell back in there and shut up."

Jack shrugged his shoulders and walked back in the vault and took up his place alongside of his son.

The phone was ringing. Billy had been expecting the call and answered with his usual, "what do you want?"

"This is Sheriff Clem Nash again. Look this has gone on long enough. I have some breakfast for you people but first before I bring it in I want to ask you something. If I come to the tellers counter in the back of the bank unarmed, are you willing to meet me there and talk this thing over?"

"Ain't nothing to talk about Sheriff. I am going to take a hostage with me and walk out the front door of this bank and get into that car that is parked there and you guys aren't going to follow me."

"I'm coming in with the food. Let's talk about it."

Billy slammed the phone down in its cradle.

Ron drove up behind the bank a few minutes later with another box of food and hot drinks. He also had a case of tear gas canisters in a wooded crate painted army green. "The guys should be taking over the barricades right now Clem. Doesn't leave very many people left to patrol the county. You sure you want to go in there again Clem? What if he takes you as a hostage?"

"I'm betting he knows, he needs me out here to make arrangements for him to get out and away. He's not going to screw that up and as for the rest of the county, it can't be helped Ron. The rest of the county will have to take care of themselves. I'm going to try once more to make contact with this guy and if that doesn't work than the shit is going to hit the fan." He took the box of food and walked to the front of the bank. Standing in front of the busted out door he paused and took a deep breath. *This is downright crazy. Why am I doing this? Because I don't know what else to do and Ron is right. He might just blow my brains out.*

Walking as if the glass under foot was eggshells, Clem went in. *He's probably watching me from somewhere in one of those offices or behind that teller's counter ahead.*

Billy had asked Jack to shut off the alarm again system once more. He stood on the top step behind a short wall watching Clem pick his way tentatively through the bank. *This is the son of a bitch who tried to poison me last night.* His gut instinct told him that if he shot the sheriff, things would get ugly in hurry, hostages or no hostages. *But damn it would feel good.* He pulled the hammer back on the pistol to cock it.

Clem heard the click as he was setting the box down. After all these years in law enforcement there was no mistaking that sound. It came from his left and he slowly turned his head scanning the wall and then saw the barrel of the revolver sticking out around the corner.

"Put the box down right there fancy pants and turn around. I don't want you looking at me."

Clem did as he was told. "I came to make a deal with you," he said talking over his shoulder. "You and your partner walk out of here right now with me and I will see that you both get a fair shake in court. The county attorney is a friend of mine and if I tell him you cooperated with me and he will look favorable on that."

Clem waited for an answer but none seemed to be forthcoming. *What the hell else can I tell him?*

"My partner is not my partner anymore Sheriff. He got what he had coming to him, but he can thank his lucky ass that's all he got. In the army they shoot traitors in the back of the head, not in the arm." The voice was sinister in an almost snarling tone. "There ain't going to be no deal sheriff. I am going to walk out of here and get in that car out front like I told you. I am going to drive away and you guys are going to sit and watch me, and I ain't telling you this again. Now I'm giving you five minutes for you to call your dogs off and then I'm coming out. You understand?"

Clem just stood there, not knowing what to say.

"God damn it sheriff did you understand or not?"

Clem did not answer him but started walking out of the bank. Plan B was next. Billy pointed the gun at the ceiling and fired blowing a huge chunk of plaster out of it and it rained down around Clem who momentarily stopped and then ran for the door expecting a bullet in the back any second but none came. He dove around the car and stared into the barrel of Ron's gun. Clem pushed the pistol to one side. "Are the keys in this car?"

Ron peered over the driver's door window. "Yep."

"I am going out back by my car. Is yours still parked there?" Ron nodded his head yes.

"Give me your keys and then start this thing up and get it out of here."

The Crown Victoria roared to life and Ron staying as low as he could in the seat, slipped it in gear and headed up the street.

Billy heard the engine come to life and ran to the tellers counter. He could barely make out the top of Ron's head but he fired at it anyway. The bullet went over the car and took out another of Adolph's store windows in a tinkering clash of plate glass to the sidewalk. Adolph, looking like a startled mercenary rose from behind the parapet where he had been snoozing before the shooting started, shouldered his powerful rifle and fired at the fleeing car. The rear window exploded from the force of the powerful rifle,. showering Ron in glass and lead fragments. Adolph worked the bolt and was taking aim once more, when the squad car careened around the corner and screeched to a stop, in the exact place where the Ford had been parked. Clem got out and walked part way towards Adolph's store, then thinking better of it, went back and sat down in the street behind the car.

Billy after firing at the car had run down stairs and grabbed for the rifle leaning against the closed vault door where he had left it. They wanted a damn shoot out, they were going to get one. When he peered around the corner again there was a squad car parked where his car had been. Incensed he fired a shot through the back fender and ran down stairs to regroup. Clem shuddered when he heard the bullet hit the car but did not return fire. He had no target and it would only bring on more gun fire.

CHAPTER TWENTY

Billy was out of control right now and the people in the vault knew it and feared it. Teddy and his Dad cowered together as if each was protecting the other. Emma hugged Ida but Ida didn't seem to realize what was happening. She continued to stare off into space. Billy walked across the vault and grabbing Debra Waters by the hair, pulled her up off the floor. "You and me are going to be leaving here my pretty friend." Then thinking he hesitated.

But wait, how and in what? They took my car away. I need to talk to that asshole sheriff again and tell him to put that car back where he found it. Upstairs now he bellowed and shoved her toward the vault door. She stumbled and fell sobbing, "please no" she sobbed out loud.

"Please don't hurt me. Please don't shoot me I have kids and a family that needs me. Oh God please don't." She rose to her feet and turned to face him her face screwed up in agony.

Billy reached out and grabbed her by the front of her dress. He had her dress bodice and her bra clenched tightly in his closed fist. He flung her flying backwards onto the steps, her dress ripping open, her bra tore in half. One of her breast was exposed and her hands went quickly to her chest to cover it.

"Nice" he smiled. "Yes, you and me are going to have a good time baby when we get out of here. Now get up those damn stairs." He spun her around and grabbing a handful of her hair, he forced the frightened woman up the stairs in front of him, but not before he slammed the vault door on the rest of them.

Clem had heard the shouting and screaming inside and was now peering over the trunk of the parked car into the bank. It was dark in the bank but he could still make out the box of food he had brought in, still sitting on top of the tellers counter. Then he saw Debra's head coming around the corner of the stairwell and up to the counter. He reached for his revolver, unsnapping the holster, but not drawing it out. At that moment Ron came around the corner of the drug store and slid in beside him.

"Where the hell is all of that noise come from he yelled?" Clem put his finger to his lips asking for quiet and pointed to the scene unfolding in front of them. "Someone is coming out," he said.

Both officers watched intently as Debra walked, sobbing towards the front door with someone behind her almost holding her up. Her clothing was badly torn and she was trying her best to cover herself but he had her right arm twisted behind her back. They stopped about ten feet from the front door and for the first time Clem was looking at his adversary. He was holding his revolver with the barrel end against the left side of her head.

Billy was glaring at Clem from behind his terrified hostage, her eyes pleading with the sheriff to do something. He looked at her torn clothing and could only guess what she had been through. His hand stayed on top of his holster but he had not drawn his weapon. Experience told him that when you resorted to weapon pointing, you were only a finger squeeze away from a battle. If the man wanted to shoot him, he'd had a couple of chances already

"I just want you to know that I am dead serious Sheriff." Billy cinched her arm tighter up behind her back and for a second she grimaced and moaned, and one breast became exposed again, but she quickly pulled things together. "Now you listen and you listen good because if that car of mine is not back here in ten minutes this little puss is going to die." Debra broke down even more when he said the word die, slumping forward but once again Billy jerked her back up straight.

"I want it put right here on the side walk and running." Billy started back where he had come from dragging the crying woman backwards with him. The two men stood there powerless to do what they wanted to do. Every fiber in their bodies wanted to pummel him into the ground but it would be a bad move. As soon as the two disappeared behind the tellers counter Clem turned to Ron.

"It's time to use the tear gas but first you need to call another Deputy to get up stairs on that building," he nodded at the hardware store, "and get that nut case of the roof. That's who shot at you, but I think, he thought it was the bad guy getting away."

"Oh good, now I feel better." Ron quipped.

Clem radioed one of the deputies behind the bank. "Tell the power company to cut the power."

"You got it Sheriff, was the reply." Over the top of the building he could see the lineman with his heavy tool belt going up the power pole.

Downstairs Billy opened the vault door and shoved Debra down on her face sliding her back into the vault. Audrey scampered over on her knees to the stricken woman and held her head to hers, trying to comfort her.

"You got ten minutes lady to get it together and then we are leaving." He looked at Audrey staring up at him. "Awe you want to go too, don't you?" Then he laughed out loud and walked back out of the vault just as the lights went out.

Clem and Ron slipped on their gas masks. The plan was to throw a couple of canisters through the front doors of the bank, wait a few seconds and then follow them in, tossing a couple more toward the back of the bank. The canisters they were using were left over World War II surplus items that Clem had purchased from the National Guard. They had practiced with them a few times and found out a couple of things that were objectionable. One was that they set the place on fire occasionally, and the other was the dispersing of the gas was hard to control, because it came out in a smoke that usually rose and everybody here was in the basement, but they had to do something.

"Let's keep them out in the middle of the room" Clem told Ron. We don't want to burn the place down with those people in it." They each lit the fuse on one and skidded them across the floor to the back of the bank. Clem's went all the way to the tellers counter across the back, skidding on the marble floor, but the one Ron threw hit the kiosk in he middle of the floor. Not where he wanted it, but no harms was done as it fizzled out anyway. They each had one more in hand and they wanted to go as far as the tellers counter and flip them behind it, but not down the stairs to the basement because of the fire hazard.

Ron's mask leaked immediately and he quit and ran out before he had gone halfway, coughing and rubbing his eyes. Clem made it to the back, but the canister he dropped back of the counter was another dud, plus Billy must have heard them walking as two gunshots came up the stairs from down below so Clem beat a hasty retreat also.

They both sat in the street leaning against the car. Ron was writhing in pain as the chemical had attacked the mucus membranes in his eyes. It was quite hot out again so needless to say there were a lot of places on his body that were wet that became effected too.

"Well that went well," Clem quipped. Ron did not answer him he was too busy rubbing all of his irritated areas.

The radio cracked and Clem answered it. It was the two deputies who had gone up after Adolph confirming that they had him in custody and what did Clem want done with him.

"Lock him in a squad until I can come talk to him," he replied.

Billy knew what tear gas was. He had seen it used in the army more than once. The first whiff of the cloud that had come part way down the stairs, sent him rushing into the vault with the rest of them, closing the door behind him but not before he sent Jack back up to turn the alarm system back on. Jack came stumbled back down; half blinded a minute later, his face screwed up in pain, tears running down his face and saliva running out of the corners of this mouth.

Billy sat on the floor with his back to the steel door staring at Debra Waters. She was sitting and crying softly into her folded arms, on top of her drawn up knees. She had apparently forgotten she had a dress on and the sight of her underpants was stoking the fire that had been lit earlier when he had torn her dress open and her breasts spilled out. *Well look at this. This girl was going to get a little of Billy's love making before this day was over and maybe it was putting pleasure before business. Well maybe rape was not really pleasurable love making, but who knows maybe she would like it.*

Audrey realized what Billy was looking at and forced Debra's legs down to the floor and tried her best to comfort her once more. She moved in front of her blocking Billy's view.

He felt himself getting aroused but them the reality of the predicament he was in, came haunting him and he got up and opened the door a crack. The gas seemed to be dissipating and it was quiet upstairs.

Ida was getting worse by the hour and right now she sat with her head on Emma's shoulder staring vacantly at the floor. Emma was still feeling very defiant. Right now, and especially after Billy's speech about shooting her breasts off, she was keeping it to herself.

As for Teddy, he had been up to go to the bathroom and he'd eaten some food and drank some water, but the truth was he was hurting bad. His arm draped at his side when he stood and his face was grimacing in pain. He tried his best to avoid Billy's eyes, casting his gaze down at the floor.

After the failed tear gas attempt, Clem had gone back to the car to get more canisters but then in a fit of frustration, he just sat down in the street.

"Watch the door Ron I am going to talk to Adolph." He got up and walked around the corner and behind the bank where Adolph was sitting in Ron's squad.

Clem opened the door to the car and told Adolph to get out. Reaching in his pocket he retrieved his handcuff key and unlooked the restraints and threw them in the car.

"Look Adolph. I want to thank you for your help but right now you could best serve your community by going home."

"That bastard shot up my store sheriff and where I come from that's reason for a man to guard his property."

"Were here to do that Adolph." Clem wiped the sweat from his face and rubbed it into his pants.

"Well you're doing a piss poor job of it sheriff-- in my humble opinion." Adolph was massaging his wrists where the cuffs had made red marks on them.

"You know what Adolph, no one asked for your humble opinion, so now get out of here until this situation is over." Clem's patience was running thin.

"Where's my rifle," Adolph demanded.

"Well get it back to you, I promise. Now scoot before I have you locked up in the county jail."

"For what?"

It was the last straw. Clem grabbed him by the back of his neck and walked with him to the street and pointed south. "Get the hell out of here and stay out of here," he shouted. Adolph walked slowly away muttering to himself. Clem watched him for a moment and then convinced Adolph was really leaving, he went back out front and sat down in the street with Ron. It was already late afternoon. It was ninety-five degrees and the sun was relentless. The two men sat in silence for some time, and then Ron spoke up.

"Look Clem, with all due respect I think we should call in the big boys."

"What big boys Ron?"

"The F.B.I. Clem. This is a federal offense."

Clem was quiet for a minute, chewing on his lower lip and staring off into space. He and Ron had been together since they were both rookie patrolmen back in Iowa City. Clem had saved Ron's life once when he was being beaten to death by a drunken giant while trying to break up a bar fight. They were as close as two partners could be and Ron was positioning himself for Clem's job when he gave it up, but hoped it wouldn't be for a while. He admired Clem to much.

Ron started in again. "It's been two days since this started and were no closer to solving it now then we were then."

"Ain't no federal Agents going to get called Ron. What do you think they would have done different then we did?" Yea, maybe they would have had some gas that would have worked and maybe they would have had some portable phones so we could talk with this asshole, but right now we haven't played all of our cards yet so were going to just sit right back down and think some more. I have a plan but it's going to take a while to put it in place." He patted Ron on the back. "Keep a close watch and I'll be back in a little bit."

He walked around the corner to the church and asked to use the phone again. There were several deputies sitting down in the basement, enjoying hot dishes and deserts the ladies had prepared. The men looked nervously at Clem wondering if he was going to yell at them for slacking off, but he didn't seem to pay much attention to them. He looked very tired and just wanted to be left alone. He called Doree at home.

He sounded tired and defeated. "I know honey what you are thinking but we are really getting close to settling this whole thing. It's just that these things take time to do right and, and."----He rubbed his eyes searching for the right words, but they were not forth coming.

Doree's reply was prompt and somewhat brash "I'm so tired of arguing with you Clem. I am tired of all of the soggy suppers, left in the oven for you that I gave to the dog the next day. I am tired of sitting at the kitchen table, my eyes searching down the lane, and wishing and praying for you to come home. Tired of going to school conferences and doctor's appointment alone, and tired of hugging my wet pillowcase at night in an empty bed, instead of beside my husband. I am tired of making excuses for you with the kids." Embarresed at her latest verbal outburst she hung up the phone softly.

She was crying again for what seemed to be the zillionth time and it was becoming almost an involuntary act. *She had cried so many nights alone in her bedroom away from the kid's searching eyes. She had thought about just cutting the cord with Clem so many times, but always that big loveable hunk would come home with that silly grin on his face and she would just melt. She could never not love him, and she knew it. Maybe it was a mistake to have found the man she loved, instead of the man who loved her. She hoped not.*

Clem looked at the phone in his hand as the line went dead. Maybe Ron was right and he was in over his head. It would be bad enough to lose the battle, but to lose Doree also? He was too tired and too hungry to think.

He went into the cafeteria and recognized Thelma and Jack sitting at one of the tables with the mayor and a reporter. He didn't want to talk to them but he knew he had to, and it better be something positive. He grabbed a cold sandwich and some coffee and sat down across from them.

CHAPTER TWENTY-ONE

Maybe they sensed that Clem was very tired and maybe they were just being kind to him but the conversation was short and to the point. Clem told them it would be all over tomorrow and they responded that would be a relief for everyone. The reporter asked about the welfare of the hostages.

"I have no way to know for sure, but all indications are that they are doing fine. We have managed to get food into them and from what we know from Jack Jr," he indicated at him with a nod of his head in his direction. "We also believe that their injuries are not life threatening."

"How do you plan to break the stalemate?" The reporter asked.

"I'm sorry but you will have to wait and see like everyone else," Clem said curtly. He went and refilled his coffee and then went outside. It was late afternoon and Ron who had been relieved for the night came around and stood by the car door while Clem drank his coffee, sitting behind the wheel of his squad car.

He reached down and shifted the car into natural. "Push it back away Ron and let's see if that door is locked."

Ron went around to the front of the car while Clem stepped out of the car for a moment. The car rolled back a couple of feet and Clem tried the handle on the door. It was locked. "Go inside the church and ask Jack Jr. for his bank keys." Ron looked puzzled. "He's that squirrelly son of a bitch that ran out of the front door yesterday when the kids were let loose." Clem nodded his head toward the church back door. "He's down there with his mommy."

When Ron came back with the keys Clem tried the door and it was locked so he left it that way. Clem explained. "Tomorrow morning when it is light, I am going to try to coax this guy upstairs and meet with him one more time. Last time he came as far as that teller's counter that runs

158

across the back. While I talk with him you are going to open this door and take him out. Just try not to shoot me."

"I noticed that there are lights on in a few places. How can that be Clem, when we cut the power off?"

"Near as I can figure those are emergency lights that come on when the power goes off. They're battery lights and I don't think they will last much longer. Yea it might be pretty dark in there soon."

"Why not do it right now while the lights still work?"

"This guy has to be getting tired Ron. Let's let him get really tired. The more exhausted we can get him, the better off we will be. If he was serious about shooting a hostage, I am sure he would have done that by now."

"Lets hope you don't crap out before he does," Ron grinned. "See you in the morning. I hope that it's over before then. I'm staying in my car tonight also, so if you need me. By the way, I hate shooting people," he added as he walked away.

Clem pushed the car back against the door and got in the back seat and closed his eyes.

Billy was exhausted but somehow his twisted mind was starting to focus again after being sexually stimulated by Debra. He couldn't get her out of his mind and he had made up his mind he was going to have sex with that woman and tonight seemed like as good a time as any. That way if he bought a bullet later on at least he would die with one more woman under his belt and a whole lot less sperm clouding his brain and poisoning his mind. He remembered when he told Teddy the consequences of having too much sperm. He had also looked at Audrey also but she was flat chested and gave him the impression of a brat and a little kid who had never grown up. He hated snotty little girls. Debra was a real woman. Maybe a weepy one, but she had the package Billy liked so much.

Then after he had satisfied his lust, sometime in the middle of the night, using the cover of darkness he was going to make run for it. Piss on taking a hostage. They would only slow him down anyway.

He started to sneak back up stairs. Maybe there was another way out of here that he didn't know about. He had talked to Jack about it but he had said no. Just the two doors and the windows you could see. But could he really believe Jack? At the last minute half way up the steps he remembered the alarm system, went back down and opened the vault and confronted Jack. "Does this alarm system work when we have no power?"

Jack looked at him suspiciously. "I--. I'm not sure, but I don't think so."

"Go shut it off anyway," he said. He watched Jack go wearily up the stairs and shut it down. Then he came back and took his place back on the floor of the vault. Billy looked over at Debra, catching her looking at him with a look of contempt in her eyes. Seeing his smile she quickly looked elsewhere still holding her torn dress shut.

Billy closed the vault door and locked it.

Upstairs he could make out the heads of the two deputies hiding behind the squad car and peering into the bank. If he stayed low, he could get into the offices on the street side with out them seeing him. They had windows that looked outside. He had no intention of using them, but he wanted to see who was watching him and he had to do it before it got dark. He pushed the office door open slowly and crawled in on his hands and knees. There were two chairs and a desk with another chair, a swivel chair, behind it. The window was right behind the chair. Lifting the blind slowly, he could make out another squad across the street and two more men behind it. There were also men on the roof of the building across the street. One appeared to have a rifle. He sat back down, his back to the desk and wearily tried to think about what he was going to do. He lifted the blind and looked out again. *They were not very good about hiding themselves. With the rifle he had, he could pick one of them off, but what good would that do him, there were many more out there that he knew of. Better to bore them into being disinterested.*

He turned around and the knob on the drawer he was leaning against became tangled in the folds of the back of his shirt collar. He disconnecting himself and then reaching back to close the drawer he saw the fifth of whiskey behind some files.

Billy handled the bottle as if he had found a great treasure. *A brand new fifth of Seagram's. Top shelf and waiting there just to be drunk.*

He broke the seal and swallowed a large gulp savoring it as it went down and feeling almost immediate comfort. *Damn that was so good.* He took another pull and lay down on the floor in silent adoration of the fiery liquid.

He crawled back out and down the stairs. He had some serious drinking to do.

Billy had finished two thirds of the bottle before it dawned on him that he had some unfinished business. He staggered to his feet, opened the door and in the dim light that was left in the vault, went over and prodded Debra with his pistol barrel. "Come with me sweetheart." His slurred voice said.

"No please," she begged and tried to push herself back in the corner away from him.

"Get up," he hissed, "before. I do it right here in front of everybody." He grabbed his crotch to emphasize his point.

"Oh God, please no" she begged breaking down into sobs once more and clung to his pants leg.

He kicked out at her to get her hands off him.

"Take me Billy" Audrey blurted out and tried to get between them.

He stared at her. It was the first time she had used his name." Get away from me you tit-less wench. Get away before I shoot you in the back of the head," he cocked the pistol and pointed at her. Audrey sat back against the wall and buried her face in her knees. The others could only watch in terror what was unfolding in front of them. Jack wanted to say something; the words were right on the end of his tongue but now was not a good time for bravery. Billy just might carry out on his earlier threat against Teddy who now lay unconscious curled up in fetal poison at Jacks side, oblivious to what was going on.

Finally Debra resigned to her fate, composed herself and stood up and starting walking towards the vault door.

"In the lunch room," Billy walked behind her; with his hand on her shoulder whispering instructions softly in her ear but not before he shut the vault door on the others.

The only light in the lunchroom was very dim, the batteries nearly depleted. Billy told her to sit up on the table. She did as she was asked and he pushed her back farther on the table and said, "Take your dress off." She did as he asked removing the dress her slip, and the remnants of her bra. She was whimpering softly but not crying anymore. He told her to lie down but not before he stood beside her and fondled her breasts. Her nipples were swollen and erect with dark areolas, as she was still actively nursing her youngest child. Her swollen breasts leaked milk from them as he kneaded them and Billy licked it from his fingers as if he had found a honey pot.

Debra could smell the rancid smell of liquor and tobacco on his breath as he leaned over her and tried to kiss her.

"Lie down," he said.

He slipped her white cotton panties down over her slender legs that she was trying her best to keep together and threw them in the corner. Then he sat down on a chair at the end of the table staring at her from her feet. He opened the bottle that had been stuck in his waist band and took another long swallow, wiping his face with the back of his hand. He seemed unsteady and disoriented and had made no attempt to disrobe himself. Debra was praying the Lords Prayer silently to herself and. praying that this monster would not make her pregnant.

She held her breath, her whole body shivering with fear. She knew what was coming and just wished he would stop gawking at her, and get it over with. She could barely make out his grinning face as she raised her head off the tabletop and looked down between her breasts. Suddenly his eyes seem to roll back and his head turned side ways and he let out a sigh. He seemed to have passed out or gone to sleep. Slowly, carefully, she pulled her knees up and got her feet clear of him. She looked for a reaction but he did not move. Slowly she swung side ways and got down off the table. The last vestige of light now glowed like a small setting sun on a cloudy evening. Her feet landed on her discarded dress and she grabbed it off the floor and snuck out of the room holding it to her chest. She had thought of hitting him with something, maybe a chair but it might just wake him up. Outside of the lunchroom, now totally dark she fumbled for the wall to find her way up the stairs. She had thought about the others in the vault but her fear of him was so strong she wanted only to get outside and tell the police that their man was asleep in the lunchroom. Then they would all be free. At the top of the stairs she could see the two officers in the glow of streetlight, standing behind the squad car and she ran screaming towards them just as the alarms went off with the last few amps of juice in the batteries. Jack hadn't shut it off and yes they did work off the batteries

The two deputies were startled at first, drawing their weapons and hiding behind the car. But this was no mad man, this was a mostly naked woman coming at them screaming "Help me, oh God please help me." In the background a klaxon was sounding but it quickly died out, ending in a bleeping sound as if a sheep was bring strangled with a gunnysack over its head.

They quickly grabbed her and pulled her down behind the car. One deputy still watched intently in the bank for whoever was chasing her, while the other one wrapped her in the blanket they had been sitting on. Then he called on the radio for Clem, who even half asleep recognized his name and quickly answered. He slipped on his gun belt and ran around the bank to the front door.

Debra was crying hysterically and trying to talk but all that came out was gibberish. Clem shook her. "Lady please settle down and tell us what is going on in there?"

"He's asleep in the lunch room," she blurted out. "He was going to rape me. "Please let me go home to my family now."

"Take her to the church," Clem told the deputy. "She needs to go to the hospital and get checked out before she goes anywhere, and by the way as long as you're back there, wake Ron up and get him out here."

He stood and peered into the dark bank. *So he had used the alarm system to warn him from intruders. Pretty shrewd all right and he'd finally gone to sleep, but why was she naked and what was he doing to her? She said he was going to rape her. Did he do it? What has he done to the others? It doesn't make a lot of sense to be this terrified of a sleeping man; she must have been put through hell. One thing is for sure this can't wait until morning we have to act and right now, dark or not.*

Clem looked at his watch holding his arm up to see the face in the street light. It was 2.15 a.m. of the third day.

Ron walked around the corner and then ran over and slid in beside Clem. "What was with that woman and what the hell is going on?"

"What we talked about last night is what is going to be going on Ron. I am through screwing around with this guy. So listen up. The alarms were going off inside when I came over here and either he shut them off or they died from lack of power. I have to believe that no one could sleep through that, but maybe the darkness will hurt him as much as it hurts us. I am going to go inside the bank and see if I can get him to show himself. You go around to the back like I told you last night, unlock that door and slip inside but not before you hear me talking to him. If you go in early you will be a sitting duck from down below."

Ron shook his head to acknowledge that he understood.

"Here's the key. Good luck."

"Why not take a couple of guys in with you?" He asked.

"The more people the more noise and the bigger chance we are going to have a shoot-out in there. Let's not have that. Now go. I will give you a minute to get back there and get ready."

The alarm going off had woken Billy. He sat up and tried to focus his eyes in the darkness. What was that noise but just as soon as it had come, it quit? His arm swept across the tabletop. *She was gone! Where the hell did she go?* He tried to make his foggy mind work. *She looked so beautiful lying there waiting so patiently for him*

He stood up unsteady, holding his hand out to feel, so he didn't run in to anything. Maybe she was still hiding here in the room. His hands felt the refrigerator door and the sink and then slid along the counter top until he felt a soft piece of cloth. He held it to his face and smelled of it. Her panties. *She wouldn't run off without her underwear would she?* He kicked over the bottle that was now lying on the floor, the rest of its contents spilled out. He bent over to reach for it and then a wave of nausea hit him and he retched. His vomit splashed into the puddle of whiskey. He waited for a moment bent over with his hands on his knees and then it came over him again and again, each time purging more of his stomach contents until there was no more. He was cold and shivering but his head had cleared.

Billy left the room and slid his hand across the wall feeling the closed vault door. It was latched. *She had not gone in there but why would she? She had gone upstairs and he had to catch her before she got outside and when he did, she was going to get both things. A bullet and a date with little Billy.*

He stumbled over the bottom step, caught himself and continued up the stairs. At the top landing there was some light from the street light out front that got inside but not enough to make out much. He reached for the pistol in his belt and then remembered it only had two bullets left in it. He went through a mental checklist. *One shot in the traitor downstairs.*

Two shots at the asshole that took his car. Where did the other one go? Ah yes that fat deputy he shot in the guts when they got here.

Billy gave thought to going down and getting the rifle but in the dark, how would he find it and it would just be more to carry. Besides he had to find her and now. *Two bullets left, one for Debra, and one for anyone else that got in his way.*

Clem had waited a minute and then as quietly as he could, while walking in the broken glass, he made his way inside of the bank. The two other trips he had made before left him with some idea about the layout inside of here. He made it to the kiosk in the middle of the floor and crouched behind it. He listened carefully but the only noise he heard seemed to be coming from downstairs and it sounded like someone puking. Then it was quiet again. He must be awake and moving around. He thought about calling out for him, but maybe he would come up on his own. Then he thought about Debra. Was he looking for her?

Clem heard the key turn in the back door lock and keyed his radio whispering hoarsely "Ron not yet."

Ron put his hand to the unlocked door to hold it from opening. He keyed his radio but said nothing. Clem would get the message. This was not the first time they had played this game communicating.

Clem waited for his eyes to get used to the dark. He had brought his flashlight but as much as it would help him see the enemy it would also help the enemy see him. Then he heard footsteps. *Shit he was coming upstairs. He sure hoped Ron did not make this the moment to open that door.*

When Billy reached the top of the stairs he hesitated. Maybe she was hiding in one of those offices.

Clem saw the outline of Billy's body for a moment and then he disappeared

Billy had gone unnoticed down the hallway to the offices that were separated from the lobby by floor to ceiling glass. He stopped to listen but it was quiet. *Maybe it was time to just make a run for it and forget about the bitch.* At the end of the hallway, in the light from the street light he saw a glass door to the left that led back into the lobby just a few feet from the main entrance door. *What had he been taught in the Army? Live to fight another day was part of it. Now! Light coming from the back of the building. They're coming in after me, but too bad suckers I'm on my way out of her. I wish I had more bullets; I would make you so sorry.*

Clem saw the light in front of him too and straightened up. Billy saw Clem and froze. Slowly the sheriff worked his way around the kiosk heading for the man in the back. Billy waited for him to go behind the tellers counter and then bolted for the door. But now there were more of them and they saw him and rose from behind the car and it was now or never. He fired his last two shots. One of the two deputies dove for the street and the other one took a bullet in his right forearm and his pistol flying across the street.

"Behind you Clem," Ron yelled

The two men turned and bolted for the front door after Billy but stopped when the shooting started and froze. Their own men could hit them. As soon as they saw Billy's head flashing by the windows on his way up the side walk they took off again out the door and seeing the fleeing man aimed their weapons but held their fire, he was running right at the barricade down the well lit street and right at another deputy.

Billy saw the squad at the road block and he also saw that no one was there, so he kept running as fast as his legs would carry him. The man who was supposed to be there had not been told anything was going on by Clem or Ron and he'd gone behind the flower shop to pee. Billy's eyes were darting everywhere looking for an avenue of escape, and looking for the allusive deputy. The storefronts were all connected and he would have to get to the end of the block. Just another few feet to safety.

Then Billy seemed to leave his feet and pitch head long into the asphalt roadway. Clem eyes saw all of this a split second before he heard the boom. He stopped and turned, looking back at Ron and the other two men, he saw one of the deputies pointing up to a shadow figure on the roof of the hardware store. In the moonlight Adolph stood holding his rifle with a night scope. Slowly he lowered it but continued standing there.

Clem walked up to Billy just in time to see his back rise one last time and then all was still. A pool of blood was running out from under him and there was an ugly hole just above his shirt collar in the back of his neck. He reached down and took the empty gun from Billy's right hand although he didn't seem in any condition to use it. In his other hand was a balled up piece of white cloth. He had pressed it to his face just before he expired. Clem opened his fingers and extracted it. It was a pair of white panties.

Ron walked up behind him and stood with his hand on Clems shoulder. The other missing deputy came running out from behind the flower shop still zipping up his pants.

Clem looked back at the roof of the hardware store and shook his head. "I thought I got rid of that son of a bitch. I took his damn rifle away from him."

Ron chuckled. "I think you forgot he sells them Clem. You have to admit that was a hell of a shot."

CHAPTER TWENTY-TWO

The beams from their flashlights bobbing through the dark preceded the men as they reentered the bank, past the broken glass and past the bloody puddles. It looked like a war zone with papers and brochures scattered everywhere. Clem and Ron where still being cautious. There was one more left in here. His brother said he was no threat, but anybody who had partnered with the nut case who lay dead in the street right now, still had to be respected. They also know there was a rifle unaccounted for.

They crept through the swinging door by the end of tellers long counter and now stood at the top of the stairs. The light from the streetlight coming through the partial open back door and a flashlight helped them see down the stairs. There was the rifle leaning against the vault door as if it was holding it shut. Two more deputies joined them coming in the back door and Clem told them." Stay up here and watch our ass boys, were going down."

Ron went down the right side and Clem down the left side one step at a time both holding their revolvers and their flashlights out in front of them. At the landing they both looked around the corner into the lunchroom area but it appeared empty. The stench of vomit, booze and rotten food permeated the air. Clem's flashlight panned the floor and there was a woman's slip and brown penny loafers on the floor next to the table and an empty whiskey bottle on the floor.

"This must be where he tried to assault her," Clem said. "I wonder where he got the booze. If I had known it would bring this to an end, I would have bought him a bottle two days ago."

"They have to be in there," Ron indicated over his shoulder at the vault door. He picked up the rifle and set it in the corner out of the way. The long steel handle that latched the door was in a horizontal position. Clem pushed down on it and the door clicked open and swung about an inch. Both men took a deep breath to prepare them, not knowing what kind of carnage they were going to see on the other side.

Ron pulled the door open while Clem played his flashlight over the five people huddled in the far corner. They were all squinting in the blinding beam from the flashlight except Teddy and Ida who appeared unresponsive. Teddy's head, in his fathers lap and Ida's head, in Emma's lap.

"It was Audrey who reacted first squealing with Joy and throwing herself into Ron's arms nearly knocking him over backwards. "Oh God were free," she kept saying over and over. "Oh I hope you shot that man. I heard shots did you shoot him, did you? Did you kill that asshole?' Ron didn't answer her question but grabbed her arms and disengaged her from himself. He asked one of the deputies that was at the top of the stairs to take her over to the church. To the other man he said, "Call an ambulance and see if you can get Doc fossum over here right away."

The vault, without any air circulating in it smelled like sweat, tears and urine. Empty food wrappers and boxes where scattered on the floor amongst bloody bandages.

Clem knelt by Emma who was sobbing softly in Ida's hair and hugging her. He knew Emma and had seen her in the bank several times. He knew Ida also.

"I'm okay Clem," Emma said wiping her face, "but she has been hit in the head and has been out of it for the whole time. Sometimes she stirs but she has been unconscious for over a day." They laid Ida down on the floor and Clem helped Emma up. "You people must have gone through hell," he said. "Go over to the church basement behind here and get some refreshments. Just don't go home yet and don't talk to any reporters yet. Tell that other young lady what I told you too."

"Butch, help her over to the church." he asked another Deputy who had showed up with an ambulance attendant.

The ambulance attendant did a cursory exam of Ida and then turned his attention to Teddy. "Both of these people need to get to the hospital right away Sheriff. Probably him first." He pointed to Teddy.

"Ok but he is under arrest so we need him put into protective custody."

"Right I will tell hospital security Sheriff".

That left Clem, Ron and Jack. Jack looked haggard but seemed to be fine. He had a large bruise on the right side of his face that was turning purple.

"That guy smack you around?" Clem asked.

Jack smiled softly. "Yea, but I'm ok. Can I go see my wife, and then can we go see our son at the hospital?"

"You're free to go, we can talk more tomorrow. Were going to need the building for a while, but when we are done we'll lock it up. You probably need to see that someone boards up your front door."

"What happened to the guy that did this?" Jack asked.

"Unfortunately, he was shot and died. Go see your wife Jack."

When Jack got outside Thelma ran to meet him and threw her arms around him. She was happier then she had been in a long, long time. "I was so worried Jack. I need you so much and now were all back together again."

Jack smiled and held her at arms length. "Let's go see our son."

EPILOUGE

Summer had come and gone and the siege at the bank in Morton was now just a memory. The Morton National Bank was still the corner stone of the downtown area and Jack Sr. still ran the ship with a steady hand. He and Thelma could be seen dining out and enjoying each others company at social functions many times a week. Jack was no longer the pompous ass he had been, but was now perceived as the town leader. He'd made plans to run for Mayor in the next election.

Teddy recovered from his wounds and faced trial in juvenile court where he was sentenced to a juvenile facility in Des Moines where he would remain until he was eighteen. His parents and siblings visited him often and he was a model student in school.

Jack Jr. was still the vice president at the bank but for some in town, he would be remembered only for his cowardly act. It was an albatross that would be with him for the rest of his life, but he bore it gracefully.

Emma retired and went to live with her daughter in Iowa City. Jack gave her the best retirement party you could ever have and an ample pension to boot. She remained good friends with the Morton family and with Ida.

Ida recovered from her head wounds but people say she was never the same. She was back working in her bakery doing what she had done all of her life.

Debra Waters and her husband and children still live on the outskirts of town. She never again set foot in that bank again, leaving that up to Doug, and she never again talked about what she had gone through.

Audrey was still snapping her gum in her bubbly manner and was now head teller taking over Emma's spot. She would talk about the ordeal to anyone who had time to listen or even if you didn't have time to listen.

The old man who had brought his life savings in the coffee can was never seen again. The rumor was he had passed away but there had never been notice of that. His shack on the edge of town had a for sale sign in the front yard.

As for Barney he was back at work a hundred pounds thinner, and without his cigarettes. He received several commendations for his bravery in the line of duty. He could be seen at the uptown café from time to time having a salad.

Adolph was charged with interfering with a police action and put on probation for five years. Clem bought a new deer rifle from him, just the other day and it just happened to be the one Adolf had used on Billy. After all he told Clem, "It was used, but it had only been shot once." They celebrated by going out and having coffee together.

Clem resigned his post as the Sheriff and Ron was the acting sheriff right now. Clem and Doree bought an implement business outside of town and right now he sold John Deere equipment instead of the law. He coached baseball for his kids and could be seen driving through town with his whole family quite often, Doree snuggled under his arm, a look of serenity on her face.

The end

CPSIA information can be obtained
at www.ICGtesting.com
Printed in the USA
FSOW01n1253300615
8409FS